F
COWIE, V.
THAT summer in S

THAT SUMMER IN SPAIN

Recent Titles by Vera Cowie

A DOUBLE LIFE
FACE VALUE
A GIRL'S BEST FRIEND
SECRETS
UNSENTIMENTAL JOURNEY
MEMORIES*

* available from Severn House

THAT SUMMER IN SPAIN

Vera Cowie

This first world edition published in Great Britain 1997 by
SEVERN HOUSE PUBLISHERS LTD of
9–15 High Street, Sutton, Surrey SM1 1DF.
This first hardcover edition published in the USA 1997 by
SEVERN HOUSE PUBLISHERS INC. of
595 Madison Avenue, New York, NY 10022.

Copyright © 1978, 1997 by Vera Cowie

All rights reserved.
The moral right of the author has been asserted.

British Library Cataloguing in Publication Data

Cowie, Vera, 1928–
   That summer in Spain
   1. English fiction – 20th century
   I. Title
   823.9'14 [F]

ISBN 0-7278-5154-3

All situations in this publication are fictitious and
any resemblance to living persons is purely coincidental.

Typeset by Palimpsest Book Production Limited,
Polmont, Stirlingshire, Scotland.
Printed and bound in Great Britain by
Hartnolls Ltd, Bodmin, Cornwall.

*This one is for Jane, who always said
I had it in me . . .*

ONE

'Miss Elliot?' Some doubt in her voice the speaker came forward, looking up at Jane with slight alarm.
'Señora de Capdevila? How do you do?' Jane stood up.
The Señora took her outstretched hand. 'So tall...' she murmured, obviously not expecting it, looking up at Jane from her five feet nothing of exquisitely dressed femininity.
'Five feet ten inches,' Jane said matter of factly.
'Your picture—we had thought—you seemed—smaller...' the Señora said delicately.
'I was not told the job called for a small person—physically or academically,' Jane said dryly.
'Oh, it does not; you misunderstand. It is just that we had thought... but it is no matter. Please do sit down.'
Jane re-seated herself on the beautifully carved straight-backed chair, whilst the Señora lost herself in an enormous armchair upholstered in soft rose brocade that emphasized the dark hair, the creamy skin, the large, heavily lashed chocolate-brown eyes.
'You wrote such a charming letter,' she said to Jane smilingly, 'and we thought you looked—' she hesitated fractionally—'charming too. You do not look terribly—"academic"—yet you are so well qualified.'

Unfolding the two large sheets of paper she carried, she took from her pocket a pair of spectacles and put them on. They gave her the look of a child dressed up in adult clothing, yet she had to be at least thirty-five; her eldest son was eighteen.

'A double first in Spanish—and let me congratulate you on your accent; it is flawless—French, Italian and German.' The Señora looked very impressed. 'I have a little English,' she said in that language, for they had been speaking Spanish. Her accent was entrancing. 'My brother-in-law speaks it like an Englishman because he spent four years at university there—at Oxford, like you.' She frowned slightly. 'I do hope Jorge will work to improve his English this summer. He is a charming boy, Miss Elliot, but he is at an age . . .' Her shrug was eloquent. 'My younger son is a natural student and my daughter, too, loves to learn, but it is not so important for her, of course.' She blushed charmingly. 'I do not mean to decry brains in women, you understand; it is just that here in Spain how a woman looks is what matters.'

'I know,' Jane said dryly.

'Ah . . . yes; you know Spain quite well, I believe.'

'I have spent as much time here as I could during the past six years.'

'You are—let me see—twenty-four?'

'Last New Year's Day.'

'But that also is Jorge's birthday!' She was delighted. 'How auspicious! Already you have a bond between you.'

Jane smiled but said nothing. From what she had been told of Jorge de Capdevila he was not the type to acknowledge any kind of bond. 'As wild as a mustang,' Professor Harris had said severely. 'Like his Uncle Luís used to be but without the strength of character to outgrow and tame it. He'll never be the man Luís is. I am afraid you will have to be strict with him ... in more ways than one.' He had looked at Jane over his spectacles and she had laughed at the twinkle in his eyes.

'... but you look as though you could deal with him very well,' the Señora was saying as Jane brought her attention back. She considered Jane, head slightly tilted like some bright-eyed blackbird. 'You are used to teaching?'

'I have had other vacation jobs coaching, as you will see,' Jane said, looking pointedly at her letter and *curriculum vitae* in the Señora's hands, 'but all with younger children. Jorge is rather older than I have been used to.'

'Ah ... yes. My dear friend the Marquésa del Puente del Sol told me you were of great help to her sons last year.'

The Señora considered Jane again, the chocolate-brown eyes soft and speculative. 'Tell me, Miss Elliot; do you always wear your hair like that?'

Startled, Jane put up a hand to the heavy coil at the nape of her neck. 'Why, yes ... usually.'

'Ah ...' The Señora seemed relieved. 'It is a beautiful colour ... and so much of it!'

'Down to my waist.'

'¡Vaya! You must look like a mermaid, for it is so fair it is almost silver.'

'I am a very good swimmer,' admitted Jane smilingly.

'Yes; you look as though you would be good at sports.'

'I am. I ride, swim, play tennis and golf. I am a good shot and I played hockey for my college.'

'¡Vaya!' said the Señora again, in wide-eyed admiration.

'It was a case of having to,' Jane shrugged somewhat

wistfully. 'My father was a great sportsman, my brother still is; I had to become one too if I was ever to see anything of them!'

'¡*Pobrecita!*' murmured the Señora tenderly, for she was a very kind-hearted lady and could visualize the little girl trying hard to emulate her father and brother.

'There is swimming at Cabo de los Angeles, of course, where we have a house right on the edge of the sea; and at Cañas, our estate in the country, we have two swimming pools, as well as horses, a tennis court and a croquet lawn, but I am afraid the nearest golf course is two hours' drive away.'

'No matter,' protested Jane. 'I can survive without it.'

Yes, thought the Señora with wistful admiration. You look as though you could survive anything. Such a splendid specimen! Tall and glowing with health and vitality, with all that amazing hair and a strong-boned, even featured face with a wide, passionate mouth. And that skin! A truly English complexion. And there was something so likeable about her; she was natural and unforced and María-José had said she was marvellous with children.

'We would wish you to accompany my younger children —Luisíto and Inés—who are twins by the way and almost thirteen—they will celebrate their birthday while we are at Cañas as a matter of fact—when they ride or swim; they are good at both but—' Again the Señora made that charming little expressive shrug—'I am an anxious mother and I would rather they had someone with them who is—'

'Trustworthy and capable,' supplied Jane.

'Exactly.' The Señora beamed at her. 'You look very capable, Miss Elliot; as though you would always be able to—to—'

'Cope?' Jane asked, in English.

'Exactly. That is the word. To cope. Such a descriptive word. And you do not look—severe. I am a tender mother, Miss Elliot. I cannot stand my children to be unduly restricted or suppressed. Childhood should be happy.'

A faint shadow of melancholy crossed her face, then she smiled brightly, 'I like you, and you come very highly recommended by Professor Harris. I am quite satisfied, but Luís . . .' She looked at her watch. 'He said he would be here but he is late. He is a very busy man, of course. Since my husband died he has managed everything for me and he is my children's guardian and trustee. I can do nothing without his consent.'

'Nothing!' Jane was incredulous. 'They are your children, are they not?'

'That makes no difference,' the Señora said wanly. 'In law it is Luís who has all the authority . . . not that he is difficult, you understand. He has been a tower of strength to me and so kind . . .'

'I can imagine,' said Jane dryly.

'Oh, please. Do not think he is an ogre. It is just that here, the men run things.' She smiled enviously. 'In England it is different, I think.'

'Not before time,' said Jane feelingly.

'You look as if you run your own life,' said the Señora wistfully.

'Well, naturally,' said Jane, surprised. 'I always have done and I always will.'

'But what will you do when you marry?'

'I shall not be selling myself into slavery,' said Jane in astonishment. 'It is a partnership surely—an equal partnership.'

'You believe in equality?'

'Implicitly.'

'Then be careful not to tell that to Luís. He is a Spaniard with very definite ideas as to the place of women.'

'The place of women!' repeated Jane in astonishment. 'The place of women, Señora, is wherever they want to be.'

'And where would that be, Miss Elliot?' The voice was vibrant, resonant, suavely sarcastic, and it raised Jane's hackles immediately.

'Luís...' the Señora started from her chair, looking behind Jane. 'I did not hear you come in; you walk like a cat...'

She went forward and Jane taking a deep breath got up and turned to face him.

He stood in the carved and gilded doorway, his head just clearing the lintel, unusually tall for a Spaniard. Very tanned, thick black hair, onyx eyes that glittered as they looked her up and down at leisure; face at once a statement and a challenge; definite bones, resolute chin, firm but beautifully shaped and humorous mouth. Broad shoulders, long legged; tremendous presence.

'Well, Miss Elliot?' The dark voice was amused, indulgent.

Jane sighed inwardly. Another one. They grew thick on the ground in Spain. 'It depends on the woman, Señor,' she said politely, not looking for trouble.

'We are talking about you, Miss Elliot.' He was equally polite but she had the impression he was laughing at her. She met the onslaught of those fantastic eyes and stood firm.

'At the present time with this household and the family de Capdevila as tutor to the three children of Señora de Capdevila during the coming summer,' she said calmly, refusing to be drawn. This job was too good to lose.

His eyes gleamed appreciably. 'Spoken like a true Englishwoman,' he said laconically. 'If Jorge is going to be a diplomat I can see your tutoring will be invaluable.'

The Señora put a hand on his beautifully tailored sleeve. He was a man women would have to touch. Jane saw this quite dispassionately. He was also the kind of man any woman would love to have touch her.

As though he read her mind he came into the room towards her. 'How do you do, Miss Elliot I am—'

'I know who you are,' Jane told him, a fine edge of sarcasm sharpening the edge of her respectful tone, which said quite plainly, 'Not that it matters.'

She met his sharp gaze blandly, and took his outstretched hand. A jolt of electricity ran through her at its touch. She felt her skin prickle, but she kept her face blank, though her heart began to race.

'Professor Harris has told me all about you,' he said narrowly: 'That you were his brightest student.'

'I have a pronounced academic bent,' Jane said with mock modesty.

'Bent?' His eyebrows rose. 'If you stand much straighter you will vanquish us all.' The jet-black eyes gleamed. 'A veritable Amazon,' he murmured and Jane knew he was laughing at her but she kept her jaw tight.

'I was telling Miss Elliot we thought from her picture she was quite small,' said the Señora brightly, gazing from one to the other, overpowered and overlooked.

'Indeed, it did not do you justice,' Luís de Capdevila said softly.

Insolent man, thought Jane furiously, but she smiled at him sweetly and said: 'Since when have women ever had that, Señor?'

The Señora put up a hand to her mouth. Jane met his haughty black stare unflinchingly and then she saw his mouth twitch.

'We go south this coming Sunday,' he said. 'Could you be ready by then?'

'I am ready now,' said Jane.

'Yes,' he murmured, *sotto voce*, 'for anything by the looks of you.'

He saw the mobile mouth tighten and the eyes, behind the tinted glasses, blaze away at him—what colour were they anyway—but she said nothing. He swung to the Señora, who had been hovering nervously. 'A word with you, Alícia. You will excuse us, Miss Elliot. You will have a glass of sherry while you wait.' It was an order, not a question. 'I will send it to you.' He took the Señora by one elbow and walked her from the room, she helpless under his grip, fluttering at his side like some moth blinded by a brilliant light.

Arrogant brute, thought Jane smoulderingly. Spaniards thought—and were raised from the cradle to believe—that they were God's gift to women and this one was obviously a true believer. Ready for anything, indeed! It did not do to come the helpless little woman when you were five feet ten inches tall and built to match; that was the sort of role the Señora and her kind played so well.

Jane had been warned by her father at an early age: 'You must learn to be self-sufficient, my dear. Women of your size are expected to be.' And she had and been thankful. She was wholly self-sufficient. She was by no means helpless, but neither was she superior. She merely liked to do whatever she did to the best of her ability, and that was considerable. She knew she could not rely on men to come to her aid; she never looked as though she needed it. She went over to the heavily ornate gilt mirror on one wall and looked at herself. No; nobody would ever take her for a helpless female. She looked what she was: strong, healthy, organized, efficient. The thick, heavy, silver-gilt hair was swept back from her strong-boned face into a heavy coil at the back of her head; she had high cheekbones above slightly-hollowed cheeks, eyes hidden behind large tinted sunglasses—she had to wear them most of the time as strong sunlight hurt her eyes. Her mouth was wide but beautifully shaped, the lips curving and sensuous. Her skin was flawless. A smooth English peaches and cream which would turn to toasted gold after a few weeks in the strong southern sun. Not pretty—no, never pretty—but alive, vividly and vibrantly alive, especially after what that odious arrogant man had been saying. And she held herself superbly; wide shouldered, long-legged. Yes, she supposed he was right; she *was* an Amazon. Too bad she did not have a spear to plunge between those broad shoulders.

A knock on the door heralded a white-coated manservant with a tray and glasses.

'*Con su permiso, Señorita.*' He brought it across to her; the tray was silver, magnificent eighteenth century, and the glasses were crystal, exquisitely cut and fragile. Oh, yes, there was money here. The professor had told her. 'A very rich, very powerful family, all under the control of Luís de Capdevila. Jorge stands to inherit a great deal. Until then his Uncle Luís hold the reins and *he* is a very fine horseman.'

Yes, thought Jane grimly, I've seen him in the saddle.

Sipping the deliciously dry sherry she wandered round the lovely, high-ceilinged room, filled with precious things. The address—in the Calle de Velásquez, in the most elegant and expensive barrio of Madrid—had told her what to expect, but even so she was still impressed by the magnificent, heavy, authentic eighteenth-century Spanish furniture, the superb crystal chandelier, the beautiful pieces of French porcelain, silver bowls filled with fresh flowers—always expensive in a country where they were not easy to grow—and most of all by the Goyas, companions to the ones she had passed in the hall. Oh, yes, there was money here all right. Everything spoke of it; all was richness and the best quality and soft-footed, soft-voiced servants. The glass from which she sipped her sherry was hand-made and struck sparks from the sunlight which came through the open window as she stood examining the Goya. An ancestor of Luís de Capdevila? The man's handsomely arrogant face had a brooding look of him.

'—And you know how Jorge is.' The voice came quite clearly through an open window, not far away, obviously from the next room, which also had its windows open.

'Indeed I do.' The deep voice was dry as dust. 'Anything in skirts is not safe within a thousand yards range. But I do not think we need worry about Miss Elliot. She will have no difficulty controlling Jorge. She is bigger then he is and therefore I doubt if he will have much success in pursuing her. In any case, he likes them small and kittenish. This one is large and tigerish and she scratches—probably bites too.'

Jane gasped.

'I think she is charming,' protested the Señora.

'That is because she wants this job. It is worth having, my dear Alícia. To live as family with the Capdevilas for an entire summer is not to be sneezed at.'

'Her references are excellent,' defended the Señora stoutly, 'and Maria-José was full of praise for the way she handled her boys last year.'

'I am quite prepared to believe what John Harris tells me about her, *and* your friend Maria-José; but I do not want her filling Inés with ridiculous ideas about women's liberation.'

'Inés is only twelve and we hardly discussed it,' protested the Señora, fighting a losing battle.

'It does not need discussing. You only have to look at her to know that this is one who considers herself the equal of any man.'

I am, thought Jane mutinously, breathing hard.

'These Amazonian females always do; it is, after all, the only attitude they can adopt since no one is going to believe they are truly feminine anyway.'

Jane almost dropped her glass of sherry. She glowed so brightly with rage she was almost incandescent. Of all the insufferable, arrogant, overbearing, male chauvinists ... She tossed off the sherry and went back to the tray and poured another one, which she downed in one gulp. It went straight to an unfed stomach, for she had overslept and skipped breakfast that morning, and was swept along the rapids of her bloodstream straight to her head. Her eyes brimmed with tears of sheer rage; the room swam in a misty, and slightly drunken, haze. She took off her sunglasses and wiped tears away with the back of her hand. Her eyes were as green as chartreuse, almost yellow in the sunlight, and brilliant with anger and humiliation. They lit her whole face with an unforgettable radiance, and as she swung round on the man coming up behind her he caught his breath. They blazed out at him out of a face that had suddenly come alive, flushed with pride and temper; a true green with little golden flecks, like a cat, and like a cat she was spitting mad.

So ... what had happened to cause this *volte-face*? Then he caught sight of the open window and comprehension flooded his own dark eyes as they met hers.

She had heard. And not liked. Ah, well ... what was

it the English proverb said: 'Eavesdroppers never hear good of themselves.' But *Dios*, she was magnificent when she came out from behind that high wall of English reserve.

'Ah, Miss Elliot,' he said blandly. 'I have decided that Jorge can only benefit no end from anything you can teach him.'

'Of that I have no doubt,' said Jane, with sweet venom, 'but surely, it is not for you to decide. Jorge is the Señora Alícia de Capdevila's son.'

'And my ward. I am also his trustee. It is I who call the tune here, Miss Elliot. Make no mistake.'

The voice was soft, the smile pleasant and she shivered at the warning implicit therein, but she was in headlong pursuit of her injured pride and vanity and did not heed the warning signs. 'What would be my punishment if I did?' she asked silkily. 'A public burning?'

The Señora drew in her breath sharply but Luís de Capdevila stood looking at Jane intently. 'I see you know your Spanish history,' he said. He was referring to King Pedro the Cruel, who, when a woman would not yield to him, had her publicly burned in the market place. 'But I think you forget yourself,' he said coldly, though she could have sworn his mouth twitched. He was laughing at her again! Devil!

'Around you—never!' Jane was seething. 'You make me only too aware, Señor de Capdevila, that I am a human being who just happens to be a woman, which makes no difference of how capable or efficient I am; the only difference I acknowledge is that of sex. I am damned if I will let you assert your superiority just because you are the opposite one. I am as capable, and as intelligent, and as efficient as any man I have ever met, and if you expect me to subvert those qualities to men just because they are men then you are wasting your time with me. The fact that I am an "Amazon" does not make me any the less a woman!'

She turned to the appalled Señora, standing by horror-stricken. *Ay* . . . Miss Jane, she thought, despairingly. You have thrown away your summer . . . and Jorge would have heeded you!

But Jane was beyond rational thinking; she was upset and wholly emotional; her great eyes were brilliant with unshed tears but her head was high and she managed to keep her voice fairly steady when she turned to the Señora and said: 'I am sorry. I have been rude, I know. I did not intend to behave so badly when you have been so very kind. I am sorry about the job. I could have worked for *you*!' The last word rang out like a church bell. And then she was gone, those long legs taking her at a great rate out of the room and out of the flat. They heard the front door slam.

Jane had reached the Castellana before she realized where she was, she was in such a state, blinded by tears and sick with horror at how she had been led into carrying out her own execution. She had lost her temper and thrown away a wonderful job. But he was such an infuriating, arrogant, cruel and heartless man. She caught her breath with a sob. This is Spain, she reminded herself. You have to make allowances. Men are the way they are here because the women make them so; pandering to their every whim, hanging on their every word, acceding to their every demand. They absorb adoration like oxygen.

She felt deflated now; the white heat of her anger cooling rapidly to a cold misery. She had thrown away the best job she had ever been offered. The chance to live like a Spanish Grandee doing all the things she loved to do—and earn a good salary into the bargain, besides finding time to finish her thesis on 'Romanticism and Cruelty in Spanish Literature'.

This exactly described that man this afternoon; cruel in his attitude and behaviour; romantic in good looks. For good looking he was; in all fairness she had to admit it. But insufferably arrogant and over-confident. Riding roughshod over the *mother* of the children. Why didn't she assert herself? Because she had been carefully trained not to, that was why. Jane answered her own question.

Because you, she told herself, were brought up by a father who never saw you as anything else but a human being who happened to be female, and who taught you to be proud of the fact; to stand tall; all five feet ten inches of you. The humour of the situation struck her then, because she had an unfailingly strong sense of the ridiculous, and she began to smile to herself, which turned into a smothered giggle, which turned into full throated laughter just on the edge of tears. Passers-by looked at her askance; another crazy foreigner; she couldn't be Spanish with that hair.

'I am glad you find us so amusing.' The voice was right by her ear and she swung round to look right at a pale blue silk tie and a beautifully cut darker shirt. Above them was Luís de Capdevila's unsmiling face.

'Yes, I followed you,' he said conversationally. 'We have some talking to do, you and I ... Come along.' Taking hold of her unresisting arm he walked her across to a pavement café, picking a table at the back, on its own, under a plane tree, where he sat her down.

Jane found her voice then. 'We have nothing to say, you and I,' she told him coldly.

'Oh, but we have. We have to discuss the programme of work you will set Jorge this summer.'

She gaped at him, open mouthed. There was a decided

gleam in the jet-black eyes. 'Why, you . . .' she burst into laughter again. Really her reactions were all shot to pieces this afternoon. 'I'll say this for you,' she said, at last, 'you have a great sense of humour.'

'Haven't I though,' he agreed affably. 'Fortunately for you.'

She met the brilliant stare. Honestly, he had eyes like a neon sign. 'I was not joking,' she said stiffly.

'Nor am I.'

They stared at each other, weighing, measuring. This was a fast-thinking, fast-moving man. It behoved her to take care; he was a worthy opponent. But Jane loved a battle; it livened things up no end. Excitement licked over her with a hungry flame; she liked a contest of skills and she had every confidence in her own. She would show him what equality was all about.

'What exactly do you want from me, Señor de Capdevila,' she said crisply.

'Now—or when you know me better?' he asked softly. She felt her face flame. He was flirting with her! Outraged, she stared at him quellingly.

'*Ojos vérdes*,' he said, inconsequentially. 'Green eyes.'

'Which do not mean I am jealous of you,' she said sweetly. Now it was his turn to throw back his head and laugh and she found it strangely disturbing.

'I think we will deal splendidly together, Miss Elliot,' he grinned.

'I don't gamble,' she said loftily.

'Oh, we will not bet on the outcome,' he said coolly.

She felt breathless again. 'Don't tell me you lack confidence in your own ability.'

He lifted his eyebrows. 'No: only in yours.'

Speechless, discomfitted, she stared at him. This was indeed an adversary worthy of her mettle.

As if he read her mind. 'Yes, it is fun, isn't it?' and then he smiled. She blinked. It was like being bathed in a sun-ray lamp. Cover him; mine eyes dazzle, she thought dazedly.

'You will handle Jorge very well,' he said crisply. 'You are intelligent, have a decided sense of humour, a quick wit and a nice sense of the ridiculous. Jorge will therefore give you no trouble.'

'You do not have a very high opinion of your nephew,' Jane commented acidly.

His face closed suddenly; became totally Spanish, very handsome and aloof. 'Jorge is very young, very handsome and very rich. He has been indulged by a foolish, adoring mother and a family who have encouraged him to believe he is above reproach.'

'A typical Spanish male,' breathed Jane innocently.

She flinched at the look he gave her.

'You have a lot to learn, Miss Elliot,' he said shortly.

'I am a very quick learner,' she assured him earnestly. She saw his mouth twitch.

'Poor Jorge,' he said sadly, 'one can almost feel sorry for him.'

'You are assuming things again,' Jane told him warningly. 'I have not accepted the job.'

'But you will, won't you?'

He threw the switch and bathed her in that white-hot smile again. There was an aura of sexual radiance about him that hypnotized, almost numbed. He was a skilled interpreter and he was translating her wishes into his will.

She was already forming the word 'No' when she met his eyes, and there was something in their depths that caused her heart to leap against her rib cage and fall back stunned. Something eternally female made her ask: 'Why should I,' in a voice she did not recognize.

'Because I wish you to.'

'Wish me to?' Really, she was as bad as he was, worse in fact; she was responding to his lead.

'Want you to . . .'

She swallowed hard to clear her ringing ears. He was a skilled interpreter all right. He had the entire picture almost before she had finished visualizing it. He was playing her; a maestro with his chosen instrument: a woman. She would upset all his plans if she refused, therefore he must see to it that she did not, and if this meant using her as a woman then it was all part of the means towards the desired end. Oh, he was ruthless all right. But, she was selling her capabilities, and so long as he bought them, how he did so was surely not important. This was only a summer job. Not a lifetime contract. And it was a very good one; too good to lose. Look how upset she had been when she thought she had lost it!

She came back to him then; not realizing that she had been looking at him without seeing him, the green eyes darker and inward-looking. His own eyes were opaque, unreadable, their flame extinguished. So was she.

'Very well,' she agreed, calm, capable, competent Jane Elliot once more. 'Just what is it you wish Jorge to improve . . .'

TWO

The road south led through the plain of La Mancha where, long ago, 'there lived one of those old-fashioned gentlemen who are never without a lance on a rack, an old shield, a lean horse and a greyhound'.

Dear old Don Quixóte, thought Jane affectionately, gazing at the ruined castles and windmills dotting the skyline here and there, a scene unchanged since the old Don had tilted at them. It was parched land; of stunted olive trees and sparse crops, dusty and yellow. Away in the distance was the church spire of the next village; behind them receded the spire of the previous one. The sky, very high, very clear, was a pale, washed-out blue above the bare brown earth; the horizon sharp and hard in the distance, the road stretching endlessly through scrubby patches of brush growing like a stubby beard among the endless dunes and hollows. The light was brilliant; a hard, white light that dazzled but was still cool at eight in the morning, the sun not yet at full power.

The big, powerful Lamborghini, the colour of a newly-minted peseta, purred its way down the multi-lane highway, Jorge at the wheel, Jane next to him, enjoying the feel of the early morning breeze in her hair.

They had left Madrid that morning at 6 a.m. so as to arrive at Cabo de los Angeles in time for lunch—around

3 p.m. It was a 550 km drive. Jane had slept overnight at the flat in the Calle de Velásquez so as to be ready for the early departure. She had met Jorge at dinner, and made a good impression.

He had been delighted with *la rubia alta*—the tall blonde, and had at once begun to call her 'Miss Jane' in the manner of a schoolboy, which he certainly was not; what he was, was a beautiful teenager with the skin of a baby, thick, dark-brown curly hair, enormous soft-brown eyes and lashes that could have been taken for fakes, so long and thick and curling were they. He was a Murillo angel boy; with a dazzling white smile and enough charm to fill the heavens, all of which he proceeded to launch at Jane, who parried his every assault in the nicest possible way, both verbal and physical, conscious all the time of the amused and satirical gaze of Luís de Capdevila. So nicely and so well had she done it that the Señora had lost all qualms she may have had at the sight of Jane's long legs and amazing hair and their effect on Jorge; they had the effect all right, but that, as far as Jane was concerned, was all they would have. The Señora was satisfied. This was a nice child; well brought up, beautifully mannered, very intelligent and vitally healthy. She would give Jorge a run for his money. So the Señora had no fears about letting Jorge drive down to the Cape in his Lamborghini, while she went in the Bentley with Luís and the twins. Jorge was a very good—if fast, driver, and in a powerful sports car there was not much Jorge could get up to, even if Jane allowed him.

Jane had expected some sardonic word from Luís de Capdevila, but he said nothing; he had seemed preoccupied, and she was irrationally disappointed.

They were an awfully nice family, Jane thought. The twins were delightful; very like their mother to look at, and not spoiled rotten, as so many Spanish children were. They had longed to ride in the Lamborghini, but their mother—and Jorge—had been adamant, each for different reasons, and they had not pushed their luck. All in all, Jane thought, she had been incredibly lucky to have landed this job. Thank heavens Professor Harris had kept in touch with an old pupil.

They had stopped for breakfast at Aranjuez, at a restaurant on the banks of the river, shaded by tall poplars, where they had eaten fresh strawberries, and delicious, still-warm *ensaimadas*, and drunk the thick, strong, milky Spanish coffee Jane loved. Now they were approaching Valdepeñas, where the famous wine came from, and soon they would begin to climb through the mountains of the Sierra Morena, crossing them by means of the pass of Despeñaperros.

Jorge had described Cabo de los Angeles, to Jane. 'It is a long, narrow peninsula, with a lighthouse at the end. On the inland side is a lagoon, always calm and still and crystal clear with marvellous spear-fishing; on the seaward side there is a fantastic beach with a tremendous surf. Do you surf, Miss Jane? I hope you do not because I would love to teach you ... there are so many things I hope to teach you this summer, Miss Jane.'

I'll bet, thought Jane dryly, but said only: 'No, I have never surfed and I would love to learn. But I am the teacher Jorge; the main lesson will be your English. From now on we will never talk in anything but English, you and I. No more Spanish. Absolutely no more Spanish.'

'Ah, but Miss Jane, there are things I wish to say to you that are not so easy in English, besides which they sound much better in Spanish.'

'English,' repeated Jane firmly. 'Now, tell me about Cabo de los Angeles.'

'Well . . . the house is right on the beach; it is white and it is almost surrounded by a high wall, with the sea at the front. From the verandah you can dive straight into the sea, at the back there is a beautiful garden which is Mama's pride and joy, with roses and carnations and jasmine and poppies and bougainvillea, and an old well where *Tío* Luís used to threaten to drop me if I was naughty.'

'Which I have no doubt was at least once a day,' said Jane teasingly.

He gave her a reproachful look. 'How could you think so,' he said, his eyes on the amazing hair, those long, marvellous legs. Spanish girls tended to have short legs. But this one was so tall. She intrigued him no end. And that hair . . . such a colour; very rare in Spain.

Jane felt his eyes on her; it was only a matter of time before he tried his hands. That was where she would have to be careful. If she treated him like the eighteen-year-old boy he was, told him to 'grow up' he would sulk and she would get no work out of him. The trick was to keep his admiration—and his ambition—in check. She was thankful her father had taught her chess. She would need to be at least one move ahead all the time.

They were climbing the mountain road now, the big car feeling no strain as the powerful engine hauled them up towards the towering red marble rocks.

'We will stop at the top and I will show you the view,' Jorge promised, and he did just that, pulling the car to the side of the road. In the distance, the snow-clad heights on the edge of Granada beckoned, and falling away below were ridges thick with a lush growth of oaks and elms, cork trees, laurels, giant thistles, and so many wild herbs and flowers that the air was intoxicating. Small mountain torrents fell down the mountainside towards the great Guadalquivir.

'Look, Miss Jane—an eagle.' Jane looked up to see it circling the highest crags.

'This is fine hunting country,' said Jorge. 'There are deer here, and mountain goats and even wolves still, though not many of them any more.'

They got back in the car and Jorge took it down the mountain and out on to the plain that was Andalusia.

They had seen no sign of the Bentley since they left Madrid. 'Luís has driven this road so many times that he does it almost automatically,' Jorge said, 'and very fast. But I am not in any hurry to come to the end of this journey with you, Miss Jane.'

Jane decided this would have to be nipped in the bud fast.

'Would you let me drive your car?' she asked, to distract him, not thinking for a moment he would. Jorge's cars were his talismans.

'You have driven sports cars before?'

'My brother's. He has an Aston Martin. He taught me to drive, as a matter of fact. He is Mark Elliot the racing driver.'

'¡Hombre!' said Jorge, face alight. 'He is your brother! But I saw him win the Monaco Grand Prix... he is a magnificent driver! If he taught you, Miss Jane, then you may drive any car of mine with pleasure.'

He was already slowing the car, drawing it over to the side of the road. Jane made to open the door and get out but he stopped her. 'No—it is not necessary. Climb over me.' His hands reached for her waist and she was pulled across his lap. He was surprisingly strong. For a moment he held her against him, then she had moved away and into the driver's seat as he moved sideways into the seat she had vacated.

'Now then ... let me see.' Jane examined the dashboard and the pedals. 'Yes ... I see ... ignition, pedals ... gear ...' She started the car, and smoothly, easily, pulled it out into the road again and slid in amongst the traffic. Under her hands the powerful car purred like some contented beast. Carefully, she increased the speed, opening up the engine, moving into the fast lane. It was a superb piece of machinery, and she handled it with ease. It exhilarated her. She had always liked the sensation of speed. Jorge thought she was like some splendid Valkyrie; what a woman! Was there nothing she would not try? She made the girls he had known up to now seem like mewing kittens. This was a woman!

After a while, ahead in the distance Jane caught sight of the Bentley. They had left the *autopista* now and the road was quieter with less traffic, though there was a fair sprinkling of the heavy lorries that one found on every road in Spain. She was content to follow it for a while, but then as a stretch of open road came up in front of her she felt the first flicker of temptation, fanned into bright flame by the sight of the Bentley sailing along so confidently.

Almost instinctively she put her foot down, judging speed and distance to a nicety. Trees flicked by faster and faster, the tyres sang, the road poured away beneath them as they crept up behind the Bentley. As they neared it Jane could see the children looking out of the rear window, talking excitedly. She could imagine it: '*Mama! Tío* Luís! Miss Jane is driving Jorge's car and she is going to pass us!'

It was perverse and it was childish, but oh ... it was so satisfying to draw level, to see the Señora's startled face and catch a glimpse of that hard, beautiful profile and a quick furious flash of those brilliant eyes, then she was past them and away, a quick mocking blast on the horn, the rush of air as they swooped past leaving the Bentley to dwindle and then vanish in the dust.

'¡*Mucho!*' crowed Jorge delightedly. 'Miss Jane you are magnificent! What a summer this is going to be...'

Jorge took over the last part of the driving because he knew the way, and it was just on three o'clock when he pulled up outside a high white wall with a high iron gate which gave on to a patio profuse with greenery and flowers, where a tiled fountain tinkled coolly and palm trees provided shade. Through flimsily white-curtained french windows the house lay, cool and inviting, with tiled floors and white-walled rooms, sweet smelling with flowers and fragrant with olive oil and garlic and freshly sliced tomatoes; lunch was ready. In front of the house, at the foot of a wide, canopied verandah, the sea lay, blue and inviting; Jane longed to take off her clothes and dive into it, and once up in her all-white room, which overlooked it, she stripped off her skirt and shirt and changed into her navy-blue Speedo. She was hungry and excited and charged with a vitality that had to be worked off. Running down the wooden stairs she ran lightly across the verandah and took a header straight in, and in a powerful crawl swam out towards the diving platform she had seen anchored about 250 yards out. She was lying there, soaking up the sun, when Jorge's head came up over the side and said: 'Who taught you to swim, Miss Jane? Mark Spitz?' She laughed and went to swipe him one but he caught her hand.

'Catch me if you can,' he invited her, and was away, as sleek as a seal and as fast.

Jane stood up and in one lithe movement was in the water, feeling it part before her, cool, yet not cold; like a caress. That last thought galvanized her and she overhauled Jorge—her arms and legs were longer—and arrived at the verandah first, placing her hands flat to vault up out of the water, when a hand came down and pulled her up. Shaking the water from her eyes she saw it was Luís de Capdevila, superbly elegant in pale blue slacks and a navy blue blazer over an open necked white shirt, a silk scarf thrust into the collar, and in a towering temper. The black eyes blazed like coals; she felt them brand her. She tensed warily, smoothing back her hair, water streaming down her, a sleek mermaid in her nylon one-piece, hight at the front, cut low at the back, revealing the superbly athletic young body, the magnificent shoulders, the endless legs. Coming up behind her, Jorge thought she looked like a water-sprite and was about to tell her so when he caught sight of his uncle's face.

¡*Hombre!* he thought, and duck-diving, beat a strategic retreat.

'Well, Miss Elliot?' Luís de Capdevila's voice was a purr but the muscles were tensed to spring. 'Have you nothing to say?'

'About what?' asked Jane carefully.

'The mad episode with the car; my idiot nephew allowing you to handle a very fast, powerfully dangerous piece of machinery at very high speed on the road that has seen more than its share of bad accidents!"

'I see,' Jane said contemptuously. 'You think me an accident risk!'

'Driving a strange, powerful car on an unknown road at high speed *is* taking a risk and Jorge ought to have known better, I admit, but you, Miss Elliot; you are no child; you should not have persuaded him.'

'And just how did you arrive at that conclusion?' Jane asked dangerously calm.

His eyes swept her up and down. 'I have seen the way

he looks at you.'

She pounced. 'But just the other day you said he would not. You said he preferred kittens to tigresses—that I had claws—and teeth!' Her eyes blazed green fire, and in ringing, passionate tones she said: "I am a *good* driver; my brother taught me and he is Mark Elliot the racing driver. I think you will agree he is well qualified to think —and say—that I drive very well. I have been driving fast cars since I was eighteen and I am *not* an accident risk!' Her voice shook with passion. 'Do me the courtesy of allowing me some level of competence! I do not do things merely because I have the fancy to do them! I do them because I know I *can*! I drove Jorge's car because I knew I could, not because I fancied I would. Why will you persist in thinking I am continually trying to *prove* something! I don't need to prove anything—to you or to anyone!'

'Liar,' he said, without heat. 'Why else did you do it?'

'Because it suited me to,' she told him furiously.

'In this family you do what suits me,' he said, in such a voice as to break out her goose pimples.

'If I do not suit the matter is easy to resolve,' she told him, still furiously. 'If you no longer wish to employ me then say so and I will leave at once.'

'You will leave when I say so,' he said calmly. Curiously enough the heat had gone out of him. He was relaxed now, and at ease, while she was the one now heated to white-hot fury.

'Why didn't you tell me Mark Elliot was your brother,' he asked conversationally. 'He is a very fine driver and I have no doubt that if he taught you he taught you well. But then'—his eyes once again measured her up and down—'you do everything well, don't you?' He turned on his heel. 'You had better go and change. Lunch is ready.'

And he left her staring after him open-mouthed.

'Oh,' she seethed, 'that—that—man! Of all the insufferable, arrogant—' grinding her teeth she took the stairs two at time and reached her bedroom breathing hard. She had a wild desire to throw something—preferably at him. Some summer this was going to be—going at it hammer and tongs with him every time they met. Why did he persist in rubbing her the wrong way?—like stroking a cat's fur up instead of down. He seemed to delight in making her loose her temper. It was a case of steel meeting steel and golly how the sparks flew! Watch out for fire, Jane, she told herself. That one has a low flashpoint and around him so do you. But all the same it was oddly exhilarating and heart-thumpingly exciting. As she brushed her hair at the mirror her faced glowed back at her; flushed with anger but alive! He had an effect on her that was pure adrenalin. All the same, it was politic to tread very carefully, so she sought out the Señora to apologize.

'I honestly did not mean to worry you,' she explained anxiously. 'I had no idea you would be so upset.'

'It was not I,' said the Señora, surprised. 'You drive very well as I knew you would. It was Luís. "That girl needs to be thrashed," he said to me. He is not used to such—independence, such—spirit, Miss Jane. But he did say you had *sal* . . .'

Jane was astonished, for this was indeed a compliment. To have *sal* to a Spaniard meant you were something more; a mixture of nonchalance and vivacity; of quickwitted responses and childish wiles; of a distinct and unique flavour . . .

The Señora was looking at her enviously. "How I envy

you, Miss Jane! So much freedom, so much scope . . . if only I had been able to do half of what you do; so naturally and so easily . . . but I was never allowed. Always guarded, always controlled . . . you are so lucky, Miss Jane.'

Impulsively, Jane bent to kiss one fragrant cheek. 'And you are very kind,' she said warmly, 'and understanding.'

'Miss Jane . . .' The Señora put one beautifully beringed and manicured hand on her arm. She hesitated a moment then said carefully: '*Cuidádo*; be careful of antagonizing my brother-in-law. He can be a very hard man and an unforgiving one. If he likes you, you can trust him with your life. You and he seem to have got off to a bad start. He is not used to girls like you; they are not . . .'

'Normal?' asked Jane dryly.

'Usual,' said the Señora firmly. 'Go carefully. He will come to accept the way you are. He already admires you . . . oh, yes, he does!' She caught Jane's disbelieving expression. 'He likes people who have the courage of their convictions; even if he does not agree with them or believe they hold the right ones.'

'As I do?' asked Jane wryly.

'In his eyes, perhaps. Give him time. You are something—new—to him. Spanish women are much more . . .'

'Subservient?'

'Obedient,' stated the Señora. 'Our tradition is that of beautiful women who run the home and look after their children; to be admired and protected and—'

'Caged?'

'Controlled, perhaps. A sweet smile, a soft glance—they can work wonders.'

'And behind the smile? What of longings and ambitions and abilities and—and capabilities? Are they to be suborned—put away in the chest with all that beautiful embroidered linen? I have not been brought up that way, I am afraid. One thing I cannot do is sit quietly and do exquisite embroidery.'

'But perhaps a little more thought before you act—when Luís is here anyway, which will not be all the time. I myself have no doubts where you are concerned; I liked you from the moment I saw you and so did my children—but with Luís...'

'I understand,' said Jane carefully. 'And I will try. Really I will. I already feel so much at home with you all... and really and truly, I only do what I know I can do.'

'And I can see that you are capable of doing a great deal,' the Señora said warmly. 'But go carefully; give him time. He will come round.'

But there was no sign of it at dinner that night. He was perfectly polite, affability itself, but somehow withdrawn. He had gone behind that Spanish formality which was as impenetrable as thick fog. There was a constraint between them. It was difficult for him, Jane knew. He had been raised in a tradition that had not changed in a thousand years; women were to be cosseted and admired; looks were what mattered. What was it the Spanish proverb said—or was it Goya...? 'A Spanish woman is a saint in church, a lady in the street and a devil in bed.' That described them perfectly.

Was that how he liked them? Devils in bed?

She must have been staring at him speculatively, because he raised his eyebrows at her and she went scarlet, looking down at her plate but feeling those perceptive black eyes on her.

Respect the customs of the country and remember you are not at home, she told herself. Do not bring shame on the Señora or the family. To be *sinvergüenza*—shameless

—is particularly distasteful to the Spanish and in their eyes that is exactly what many modern women are. Perhaps he is old fashioned and that is what he does not like.

A lady in the street... and a devil in bed. It kept coming back into her mind. He was certainly attractive enough. Why wasn't he married? Fussy—or fanatical? Surely he had girl friends somewhere. Perhaps even a *novia*. He was much too handsome and masculine to be living a monk's life. She would have to keep her eyes open. It would be interesting to see just what kind of a woman attracted Luís de Capdevila. But in the meantime she wished she could show him that she was not engaging him in a fight for supremacy; that she was as she had been raised, by a practical, pragmatic father and an impatient older brother: if she wanted to do a thing with them, fine, but learn to do it properly.

Luís went back to Madrid the next afternoon. Jane was rather relieved to see him go, but was surprised to find that she kept thinking of him during the following days, while they established an easy routine. In the mornings, after breakfast, two hours with Jorge to work on his English, and she kept him hard at it—and at arm's length. No easy task. Jorge had set his mind on achieving his aim with Jane and was totally single minded in that direction.

She was therefore relieved—as well as surprised—to see Luís de Capdevila sitting on the verandah on Friday afternoon when she and the children came back along the beach from a shell-collecting expedition. Jorge was always more circumspect when his uncle was around.

Luís stood up as they came along the verandah. 'Good afternoon, Miss Elliot.'

The children shrieked with laughter. 'We do not call her Miss Elliot, *Tío* Luís! She is Miss Jane.'

'Very well. Good afternoon—Miss Jane.'

Her name on his lips gave her a funny frisson down her spine.

'You did not say you were coming,' Inés said. 'Why did you not tell us?'

'All the better to surprise you,' he said lightly, holding Jane's eyes; his were not unfriendly, like his smile, so she relaxed a little.

'How long are you staying?' asked Inés. She was a little girl who liked her facts straight.

'Until Monday morning.'

'You never usually come at weekends.'

'I cannot usually spare the time.'

'But you are sparing it now,' Inés pointed out practically.

'Don't you want me to? Shall I go back to Madrid?'

'No! No! We want you to stay. Don't we, Miss Jane?'

Jane met the gleam in those onyx eyes. 'Do you Miss Jane?' The voice was dulcet.

'Oh, indeed,' her own voice was just as sweet, but she was surprised to find it was true. His presence added excitement; spice to an already highly-flavoured existence. More battles, perhaps? She found she had enjoyed the ones that had gone before. Had he? He must have. Why else had he come down?—Inés had said he did not usually come at weekends, and 1100 kilometres was a long way to drive in three days. Unless it was to check up on her; to see she was not making a disciple of Inés in the religion of total equality. But there was always the telephone. He had no need to check personally. Or had he?

Now hold on there, she told herself. You are jumping at conclusions like they were free gifts. His reasons are his own and why should they be important anyway . . . ? He is here, that must be enough. He works hard and needs a break; it is summer after all. He has probably come down to rest.

But he did not rest. He came with them when they went swimming, and he took them sailing in his catamaran. He even went with Jane and the children when they went over to the other side of the peninsula so that Luisíto, who was going to be a marine biologist, could collect specimens; was happy to wade through the rock pools collecting crabs, sea urchins, anemones, algae and tiny fish. It was he who found the seahorse. He called to Jane who was nearby.

'Look—how lucky—a *caballo del mar*.' He held it cupped in his hands; a tiny, extraordinarily elegant, pale-green creature with a definite horse's head.

Jane caught her breath. 'Oh,' she exclaimed softly. 'How perfect!'

'You have never seen one before?' He was surprised.

'They don't swim around in the North Sea,' Jane said ruefully.

Luisíto came across to see what they had found.

'Quick, Miss Jane—a plastic bag.'

Jane got one and half-filled it with seawater, spreading the neck of the bag wide so Luís could pour the tiny creature into it. Gently he tilted his cupped hands so that the water, and the seahorse, ran into the water-filled bag; as he did so his fingers brushed Jane's and she jerked the bag.

'Be careful Miss Jane,' scolded Luisíto, and hot-faced, very careful not to look at Luís, Jane fastened the plastic bag with a strip of plastic wire before taking it over to where they had stored the rest of the specimens; a big wicker basket. She spent some time unpacking and repacking it before returning to the rock pools, this time on the other side of the bay.

And he came with them to the *feria* in the village, and ate hot *churros* and ice-cream and watched Jorge and Jane compete for a bottle of champagne at the rifle range, which Jane won, and then took on the winner in a 'reigning champion' duel—which he won.

'Just,' said Jane challengingly.

'You have a good eye, Miss Jane,' he admitted, and that gleam was back in his eye: 'two very good eyes.'

Startled, Jane met that gleam and turned away, feeling rather dizzy.

On the Sunday, a brisk wind was blowing and Jorge went across to see what the surf was like. Too rough, he reported back—'but fantastic for swimming, Miss Jane. You dive into the roller as it is about to break. What a sensation! You must try it.'

Jane looked at Luís from under her lashes.

'You are a strong swimmer, Miss Jane, but it is not for fainthearts...'

That did it.

'Or for children,' called the Señora firmly as they left...

It was exhilarating; noisy but exhilarating. The rollers thundered in like stampeding horses and the trick was to judge the moment so that you dived into but came out through it. Several times she misjudged and ended up being tossed like a cork on to the beach, winded and gasping. One of them was so big, it picked her up, swamped her and rolled her, blind and helpless, into some other body and tumbled them, like washing in a machine, over and over in a tangle of arms and legs, on to the beach, laughing like lunatics. And it was Luís.

When he left after breakfast on the Monday morning Jane was at once peculiarly sad and glad; she could not sort out exactly just what she wanted, but as the week went on she longed passionately for the weekend to come and knew that without doubt what she wanted was to see him. When, on the Friday night he still had not come she was so miserable she had difficulty in not bursting into tears. But on the Saturday morning when she came down to breakfast, there he was, sitting at the table drining coffee and reading the paper, and her stomach turned over and she was slightly breathless as she said: 'Oh, hello! When did you get here?'

'About an hour ago.'

'You drove all night?'

'Of course. I like driving at night; it has a special sort of magic—and the roads are quieter.'

'But aren't you awfully tired?'

'Not any more.'

And she felt the glow spread through her like a forest fire.

But apart from the physical delight of his presence, he was a marvellous companion. The children adored him; obeyed him without question and trusted him implicitly. They knew just how far they could go before the velvet glove came off and the steel showed, bright and hard.

The Señora deferred to him in all things. Like the children he had her complete trust. Only Jorge fought the curb and it was only himself he hurt.

With Jane he was easy, charming—oh, how charming; almost before she knew it her heart had left her body and was pinned, bright and shining, to her sleeve. She in turn was very careful not to hurl herself at that iron will. They both, with tacit but unspoken understanding, kept well away from the forbidden subject, though Jane always gave of her best, no matter what she did.

Watching the way she melded with the children the Señora knew that Luís's professor friend had been right;

this was indeed a remarkable young woman who was, as if by some unseen hand, being turned into a very lovely one. The smooth, rounded limbs, tanned by the sun to an apricot gold, glowed with health and exercise; the silver-gilt hair, washed daily to rid it of salt, for she never swam with a cap, was soft and shining, the great cat's eyes glowed with a soft light that came from within and illumined her whole face with a radiance that caught the breath. She moved, too, with a fluid grace that was all the more eye-catching because it was quite unstudied.

Jorge was dazzled. 'Miss Jane, you are blossoming like mama's roses,' he said one night, when she appeared for dinner in a floating chiffon dress the very colour of those flowers; all soft roses and muted pinks and creamy creams. She turned on him a smile that was sweet though dimmed; it was under Luís eyes, when he came in and looked at her, that the tightly furled bud opened fully, turning to the sun, which was his presence.

The Señora was troubled. Luís was a stunningly attractive man, but he was not an easy one. Miss Jane could get hurt. An accomplished flirt, he was no easy match for a 24-year-old girl coming alive before their very eyes, and responding to his practised charm with a totality that was terrifying.

Luís was no philanderer and his sister-in-law had never known him deliberately to set out on a course of seduction, but he had been coming down to Cabo de los Angeles more than he usually did. An odd weekend had been his usual ration until August; he had now been three weekends in a row—and this was an extra long one again.

Miss Jane was enchanting, of course, especially now, and she was great fun and so likeable. Effortlessly and athletically graceful she was a joy to watch in and out of the water, and the Señora had seen Luís doing just that.

Jorge did too, of course, but Jane could handle Jorge. Luís was another matter; he had twenty years more experience, usually with women very different from Miss Jane; older, more sophisticated; like Queta dos Santos, for instance; beautiful, supremely elegant, always immaculately turned out, hair and clothes a consummate work of many hands and much time. Not for them the stained and faded denim jeans or shorts, checked cotton shirts, long bare legs in grubby white sneakers, hair tied back in a careless pony tail except in the evenings when she wore a pretty dress for dinner; then she wore it in a thick coil behind her head. They were no longer 24 years old, of course; not now able to go around with a face bare of make-up, or able to let their immaculate coiffure get soaked for hours at time then wash it under the shower and let it dry to a thick fall of silver gilt which Inés loved to comb and dress, plaiting it and then threading it with flowers; magenta geraniums, scarlet carnations, red rosebuds and purple bougainvillea. The Señora had caught the sudden, unguarded look on Luís's face one evening as he looked at Jane and had trembled inwardly.

There was something—not withdrawn, but withheld, about Luís these days; as though he watched and waited under an intolerable restraint. He was never anything but perfectly correct with Jane; he teased her and amused her, talked and listened to her, always with great interest. The two of them had apparently buried the hatchet; they were each careful not to draw steel, and had grown into an easy, mutually satisfying friendship but—and especially on Jane's part—the Señora saw this change subtly as her awareness of Luís as a desirable and attractive man increased her own awareness of herself as a woman and, in consequence, her own desirability.

It was all very disturbing to the Señora, though her

confidence in Luís was absolute. He would never do anything to hurt, or spoil, or leave a nasty taste in the mouth. He did not trifle. That was not his way. What then, was his purpose in coming back so often to Cabo de los Angeles? What was it about Jane, apart from her slowly unfurling beauty and desirability? What did he want? Was it Jane? She was so much younger than he was. Luís was 38; women had always pursued him and he had taken his pick as and when he wanted to. But the Señora sensed that with Jane, all was not as easy or straightforward as those other times. It troubled her, but she knew better than to say anything to him about it. She trusted him and all she could do was wait and see.

So the days fled by. Jane worked steadily every day with Jorge, and true to her word never spoke or listened to him except in English. The same with the twins, and as the summer went by their fluency and their accents improved. The Señora loved to lie out on the verandah listening to the chatter of Miss Jane and the children as they all laboured to make an enormous sandcastle, with battlements and a draw bridge, all surmounted by paper flags that fluttered in the breeze; or laid out a shell garden, or played in the sea, or dived for *pesetas* in the window-clear water of the lagoon. Miss Jane was a treasure.

Jorge she always kept at arm's length. It was difficult at times, for as she bloomed so did his ardour; he was always trying to insinuate an arm around her waist, a kiss on her nape, trying to slide his mouth across her cheek to her own mouth. She would never let him get her alone; she went with him to parties in the houses of his friends, sailing with a group of them, to a barbecue on the beach, but as he grew increasingly amorous and frustrated so did she refuse to put him out of his misery.

The weather was perfect; day after day of cloudless

skies and hot sunshine and a flat, placid sea. The people of the village came to know and like *la inglesa rubia*; her easy command of the language and love of all things Spanish they took as a compliment to themselves and appreciated as much as they did her. She very soon got to know the fishermen, and the jovial couple who ran the only village shop, a paradise of fragrance because it sold everything from string to salt-cod and was festooned with strings of garlic and dried herbs and spicy sausages like *chorizo* and *butifarra*; with *jamon de serrano*, with cheeses and fresh fruit, from the delicious *chirimoya* with its indescribable taste and shiny black seeds to great green melons and bunches of sweet grapes. She went with Antonia the cook on her early morning forays to haggle with the fishermen for crabs and tunnyfish and tiny shell-like *chirlas* and *almejas*, and *calamáres*.

She enjoyed everything with an instinctive, unalloyed delight that endeared her to everyone. She appreciated Spain and its way of life to a degree that made Luís de Capdevila say teasingly one night at dinner, 'I think you must have a Spanish soul, Miss Jane.'

She took him seriously. 'I sometimes think I have,' she said. 'I never have felt as if I was in a foreign country and I do think of Spain as my second home.'

'You would not mind living here in Spain—for always?' He watched her intently.

'Oh, no! I'd love it. No problem.'

He raised an eyebrow. 'No problem'?

She met his eyes then lowered her own to her plate. He was mocking her again, but nicely. 'Well ... there might be one or two,' she allowed cautiously.

'Such as?' he pursued.

She slid him a look from under her lashes. 'I should probably never be able to get used to having to ask before

I did anything.' She lifted her head to look at him directly. 'I am used to doing first and explaining afterwards.'

'Ah,' he said, 'a law unto yourself?'

'No,' she corrected. 'Just an individual.'

'It is important to you—to be yourself and not just an—appendage?'

'Of course,' she said innocently. 'I am myself. Everyone is an individual with their own minds and personalities and rights...'

'Ah, yes,' he said, 'rights.'

Jane looking mutinous but mindful of their new relationship said nothing.

Later that night, she lay out on the verandah listening to Julian Bream playing the *Conciérto de Aranjúez* and watching the enormous Spanish moon, blood-red and glowing, as it sat on the horizon, dreaming up at the night sky ablaze with constellations never seen in England; diamonds of the first water strung out into necklaces of a size and brilliance that dazzled. The children were in bed, the Señora had gone to visit and gossip with friends, Jorge was somewhere else with his and Luís de Capdevila had driven off somewhere in the Bentley.

Although it was one o'clock in the morning, it was still very warm, the sea a plate of black glass, the moon's reflection a shiny ladder of sequins that stretched to the horizon. Jane lay supine on one of the deeply cushioned loungers and listened to the romantic music and thought she had never been so happy. But unconsciously her hand played with the long silken lengths of her hair, dreamily and sensuously, and she sighed now and again. She felt she was floating; the combination of the moon, the stars, the warmth and fragrance of the Señora's flowers, all combined to wrap her in a deep, warm romanticism.

Yet she somehow felt incomplete. Something was missing. She was content yet not wholly satisfied. She sighed again, stretching her hands above her head, like a cat uncoiling itself, feeling her body tense before she relaxed it slowly and completely in sensuous abandonment.

Coming in silently through the back of the house after parking the car Luís de Capdevila heard the music and went to investigate and through the sheer curtains saw her lying there. In the moonlight her hair was a silver-gilt waterfall streaming over shoulders bared by a halter-necked cotton dress that exploited their satin smoothness; her long legs and feet were also bare, just as smooth, just as gleaming, and she had her eyes closed and a little half-smile on her mouth as she lay in an attitude of almost abandoned langour, wholly caught up in the music, the beauty of the night and her own imaginings. The guitar dripped honeyed notes like golden teardrops into the heavy, sweet warmth of the night air and he saw her hand go to her hair, twining and caressing and smoothing, its silken heaviness gleaming as it caught the moonlight. He heard her sigh, saw her rub her cheek against the cushion as though against another cheek, then move her head restlessly. Suddenly, as the guitar began to throb passionately, she was out of the chair in one convulsive movement and had stripped off her dress. Underneath she wore only her backless swimsuit. She took two steps, did a beautiful jump-dive that parted the water almost without sound and he saw her reappear way out and streak away towards the platform in a powerful crawl. He watched her until she disappeared.

Jane swam until she was exhausted, trying to escape from the enervating lethargy that weakened and loosened her. She was tired when she came back and knew that now she would be able to sleep. As she neared the house she heard the music again, dreamily romantic, and felt the waves of longing sweep over her again. Turning on to her back she floated, her hair sweeping out behind her like some sweetly innocent Ophelia, eyes closed, arms outstretched. Inside her was an ache like a stone; it weighted her spirit and filled her with a sweet melancholy she had never known before. Tears flowed silently and dripped down her cheeks into the water.

What is the matter with me, she thought despairingly. I'm drifting and mooning about like a lovesick calf... I am sick. Sick of love. Sick of an old longing. For Luís de Capdevila. I love him, she thought. I am in love with Luís de Capdevila. Oh, God, she thought, now what do I do? As if in fright, she kicked water, turned over and in half a dozen strokes had reached the steps, placed her hands flat on the matted surface and in one easy movement vaulted up on to the verandah. And there stood Luís de Capdevila with a large towel in his hands.

'Oh,' she gasped.

He handed her the towel. 'Moonlight swims should not be undertaken alone, Miss Jane,' he said expressionlessly. 'Even powerful swimmers like you can get cramp.'

'I'm sorry,' she said, flustered. 'I didn't think—'

'How unusual,' he commented dryly.

'It was an impulse,' she explained confusedly. 'I just felt—'

'I know how you felt,' he said calmly. 'Nights like this and a moon like that can have a powerful effect. Southern Spain on summer nights can be a potent aphrodisiac...'

Even more alarmed and confused Jane began to rub herself down with the towel. I don't need the moon, she thought. You are quite enough for me...

She shivered.

'You are cold?' he asked sharply.

'No... no... the water was beautifully warm—like silk...' Her voice trailed off and she flushed and applied herself concentratedly to her drying off.

'You like Spanish music, I see,' he said, as the *Conciérto* came to and end.

'I like everything Spanish, you know that,' Jane murmured shyly.

'Everything?' His voice was deceptively soft and her stomach fell to the basement.

'Everything,' she said, as calmly as she could. Turning her back on him she went to wring out her hair over the edge of the verandah. He leaned against the balustrade and watched her.

'You are enjoying your summer, Miss Jane?'

At that she turned to him, impulsively. 'Oh, yes, very much. I don't know when I've been so—'

'Happy?'

'Yes. You have all been so kind to me...'

'You have been—good—for us. I am glad we got over our—initial differences and you decided to—take us on.' His voice was urbane, slightly mocking. 'Jorge and the twins will be completely bi-lingual by the end of the summer. You have done very well, Miss Jane. My old friend John Harris was so right to recommend you to me.'

Jane flushed with delight.

'I have done my best,' she said shyly.

'Which is considerable,' he said dryly. 'What will you do when you back to England,' he asked idly.

'I have a thesis to finish—some postgraduate work. I had intended to do some work on it this summer but—' she shrugged ruefully.

'There are other things to do,' he agreed smilingly. 'What is your thesis about?'

'Romanticism and Cruelty in Spanish Literature.'

'Indeed!' He raised one eyebrow. 'And what would you know about either?' he asked softly.

'In literature—a great deal. I have read it all.'

She wrapped the towel about her waist like a sarong, quite unconscious of the picture she made with her hair streaming down her back, the towel emphasizing the swelling curve of her hips, the wet suit clinging to the high firm breasts and exposing the long line of her bare back.

'Books are one thing,' he said . . . 'Are you a romantic, Miss Jane? I think you must be; the *Conciérto de Aranjúez* and moonlight swims and water like silk . . .'

His voice was like the water and she nervously put up a hand to smooth back her hair; a drop of water ran crookedly down the silvery smoothness of her arm from her wrist to hang suspended, like a teardrop, from her elbow. She was microscopically conscious of him with every hair on her body. An all pervading tingle crackled all over her and hung between them like high-tension wires.

'It's late,' she faltered. 'I must go to bed . . .' Oh, God, she thought, that was the wrong thing to say . . .

'It is not late for Spain, Miss Jane,' he reproved, turning to look at the moon. 'In Spain we call this a lover's moon—*la luna de amor* . . .'

'We don't get that sort of moon in England,' Jane said trying to be matter of fact, failing hopelessly.

'Perhaps that is why you are so unromantic—as a race, I mean. Not you.'

She felt her heart stamp its feet. How long had he been watching her? What had he seen? She had not given herself away . . . suddenly she was terrified. For heaven's sake, she told herself irritably. How could you . . . moonlight and music can mean a lot of things . . .

She turned to pick up her dress and sandals. She found

one but the other had gone under the chair. Stooping, Luís de Capdevila retrieved it but made no attempt to give it to her.

'Yes,' he said musingly. 'I think you must definitely have a Spanish soul.'

'And an English set of opinions,' Jane said crisply, desperately fighting her way out of the web he was weaving.

'Is it possible for the two to go together?' he wondered. 'I should think it would make for constant friction.'

Like you and I, she thought achingly.

'But then, you like arguing, don't you?' he asked dryly.

'It can be—stimulating,' she agreed, cautiously.

'Yes,' he said dryly, 'I know.' His voice raised her goosepimples.

'You hold very definite opinions, don't you?' he asked next and she sensed he hung on the answer.

'On some things, yes.' Her chin went up at once.

'Unchangeable?' The voice was deceptively soft, the eyes watchful.

'Until I see reason to change them.'

'Ah . . .' It was like a caress. 'Then you are capable of seeing reason?' Again the silky mockery. He was baiting her again.

'I trust I am capable of seeing a lot of things,' she answered stiffly.

'Oh, I know you have two good eyes,' he said. Then his voice changed. 'Remarkable eyes; like a cat. As green, and as beautiful.'

Jane gulped. She did not dare to look at him but she was skin-crawlingly conscious of him standing there; of the gleam in those unfathomable eyes, the fragrance of sharp-sweet cologne and tobacco, of the long-fingered hand holding her sandal. Awareness suddenly hummed between them. She found she was trembling and it was in her voice as she asked politely: 'If I may have my sandal, please?'

He smiled and she blinked. 'It is not a glass slipper,' he said amusedly, 'but then, Cinderella was far from being liberated, was she not?'

He was laughing at her again. She eyed him smoulderingly.

'I buy my own shoes,' she said pointedly, 'and besides, glass is extremely impractical as well as uncomfortable.'

He laughed. 'And to think I called you a romantic.' He raised one eyebrow. 'In that case you will surely wish to put on your own shoe . . .'

She had not intended to wear them but his words were a challenge. She held out an imperious hand.

'If you will give it to me.'

Their eyes met and locked. Silently he held out the sandal in such a way as to brush her fingers when she took it. She flinched as if from a branding iron and shakily bent to put it on, but she was in such a state she could not get her foot through the narrows straps.

'Allow me,' he said politely, and bending down picked up her foot with one hand and put the sandal over it with the other. Jane sank her teeth into her lower lip and forced herself not to quiver convulsively at his touch. He took the other sandal from her unresisting fingers and put it on the other foot, then he straightened. They stood staring at each other, awareness of each other strung out to an unbearable tension.

Jane knew a sudden wild and irrational desire to take the two steps that would bring her close to him, put her arms up around those broad shoulders and kiss that taut, unsmiling mouth; something, she realized achingly, she wanted to do more than anything. She was almost sick with the stomach-churning excitement he was generating, and she closed her eyes and swallowed convulsively.

When she opened them again he had stepped back and away from her, out of reach.

'Good night, Miss Jane,' he said politely, impassively, secure again behind his impenetrable Spanish formality.

She did not realize that her eyes, her expression, gave everything away, that what Luís de Capdevila was doing was not what he wanted to do and that it took all his control to do it.

Her throat was thick and her voice dead: 'Good night,' she said and fled.

In her room she leaned against the door and trembled so much her teeth chattered. In one swift movement she stripped off the towel and the swimsuit and flung herself under the sheet as if to hide, curling herself into a ball to try and control her shaking body. She couldn't. Turning on to her back she forced herself to take deep breaths, to relax the tension that had her knotted like string. Through her open window she heard the scrape of the chair, the flare of a match, the creak of the springs as he sat down. Pushing her face into the pillow she said his name against it, over and over again. She felt again the touch of those fingers on her ankle and foot and her mouth dried and her body melted. God knows what she would have done if he had kissed her. Gone to pieces, probably. Fragmented like a star-shell... the thought of that mouth on hers was enough to turn her to jelly; all loose and pliable like putty. Had he wanted to kiss her as much as she had wanted him to? She still did; the ache was still there, worse than ever, unsatisfied, churning until it was almost a physical nausea. She ran her fingertips over her mouth, imagining they were his mouth... never in her life had she been so physically consumed by desire; so conscious of any man. Just to look at him was a pleasure almost too exquisite to be borne ... she could not stop wondering what it would be like to be held in those arms, against that strong body, her mouth under his mouth, opening to receive his kiss ...

She thrashed about the bed in anguish. She knew the feeling was mutual; that he had been as conscious of her as she was of him. But he had not crossed the drawn lines; not taken that step that would have irrevocably changed their relationship. Why? Why? Was she imagining things—reading signs wrongly, grasping at implications that had no substance in reality? Surely not. At twenty-four Jane knew enough to know when a man found her desirable; she had been conscious of that fact with Luís de Capdevila for some weeks now. Yet he never deviated from his flawless politeness, his subtle teasing, his mocking amusement. Was it because, deep down, he did not approve of her—of her opinions, strongly held beliefs and way of life? Was his disapproval stronger than the attraction she held for him?

She churned around in bed trying to find answers, every one eluding her. She knew it would be even more difficult to be at ease with him from now on; the physical attraction between them made it impossible for them to continue in the same, easy way. She was too conscious of him; of the way his hair grew, of the onyx eyes that could gleam with so many expressions, of the firm yet sensual mouth, of the long fingers that she longed to have caress her, the breadth of his shoulders, the long legs. The feelings she was struggling to contain threatened to burst their straining bonds and she did not know how long she would be able to hold them in. And there were six more weeks to go. It would be best in future not to be alone with him; best if he did not come so often, though the thought of not seeing him was an unsupportable anguish. Oh, God, she thought miserably, what am I to do? Burying her face in the pillow she cried herself to sleep.

Next morning, when she came down to breakfast he had gone. Left a day early.

'He is a busy man,' said the Señora shrugging. 'And he has been down here a lot lately. Now he must catch up on things...'

She eyed Jane's drawn face. When she had returned last night she had found Luís sitting on the verandah and knew from the expression on his face that he was in one of his moods. He was curt and abrupt and somehow on a short-leash. She knew him well enough to know something had displeased him and one look at Miss Jane was enough to tell her what it was. Things were coming to a head between them. She had seen it coming. It was best he should remove himself. That way Jane would be able to regain some measure of stability. She was totally at a loss to deal with her own feelings; without the tormenting presence of Luís she would perhaps be able to sort them out, to come to terms with them. The Señora longed to be able to say something, to comfort the desolate, unhappy young girl. She felt unreasonably cross with Luís for causing it all. What was he thinking of? It was not like him to allow such a thing to happen. Was it because he was not able to stop it? The Señora sighed. She wanted things to go on as they were; Miss Jane was a treasure. Jorge and the children adored her, she had no worries where they and Miss Jane were concerned— but Luís... She had thought from the beginning he seemed more than casually interested in Miss Jane Elliot; he had gone to unusual lengths to persuade her to take the job. And he had spent more time than he ever had down at the villa. Why? Was he serious about Miss Jane?

She was sensible girl and surprisingly adult for a twenty-four-year-old but Luís was thirty-eight... It was out of character for him to set out deliberately to fascinate a girl so young and so—inexperienced. Was it because she was so unlike any other woman he had met; so matter-of-factly sure of her own capabilities; so candidly and frankly at ease with her own liberated view of life? So different from the docile and totally dependent Spanish women he was used to.

The Señora sighed. She hoped Luís would stay away for a good while so as to let things simmer down. It would be best for all concerned. Perhaps it was only a summer flirtation; a consequence of being thrown together, of close proximity and a mutual physical attraction that went no further than that. The Señora hoped so. She did not want to see Miss Jane hurt. And that again was not like Luís.

Oh, it was all too complicated and disturbing. Best to wait and see and let things take their own course.

And then suddenly, they had been at Cabo de los Angeles eight weeks and it was the Feast day of *Nuestra Señora de los Angeles*. The *pueblo* was en fete. After that they would leave for the last month usually spent at Cañas.

The children were all excited.

'There is dancing in the plaza, and all the fishing boats are dressed with flowers and flags and they make a procession round the harbour and then the *Virgen* is carried to the church and there is a High Mass and afterwards there are fireworks and music and wine and everyone has a wonderful time,' babbled Inés. 'We will show you everything, Miss Jane.'

Jane had hoped the 'we' would include Luís but in two weeks there had been no word or sign of him. He did not come that Friday, or the Saturday, when the *Fiesta* was held, and though she watched the procession, attended the High Mass, applauded the fireworks and danced in the plaza, drank lots of wine and was gay and light-hearted outwardly, inside she was hot and feverish, poised on the edge of a peak of frustration with a sheer precipice and a bottomless drop.

It was three in the morning when she and Jorge came back from the dancing, hand in hand along the edge of the sea, Jorge carrying Jane's sandals, her bare feet scuffling sand still warm from the long day's sun. As they strolled, she felt Jorge's hand leave hers and slide round her waist, but she did not care. It was a glorious night, brilliant with stars, and as they neared the house she could smell the Señora's cherished flowers; the sweet, heady fragrance of jasmine and roses and the herbs that grew in pots: rosemary and thyme and borage.

She was floating; adrift on a sea of wine and longing and misery. Her feet seemed not to touch the ground, and when, just in front of the verandah, Jorge took her in his arms and proceeded to kiss her, as he had longed to do all summer, murmuring passionate declarations and caressing her tremblingly, she just stood there and let him, not feeling, not hearing: a dead thing.

When finally he let her go, to look at her in sad reproach and say resignedly: 'I am not getting through to you, am I Miss Jane?' all she could murmur distractedly was: 'I'm sorry, Jorge . . . I had a lovely time really . . . it's not your fault . . . thank you for taking me . . .' and did not even notice when he had gone.

She felt very strange; not drunk, but high—definitely off the ground. Drifting up on to the verandah she wrapped her arms around one of the pillars and dreamed up at the fantastic night sky. Lifting languidly heavy arms she unpinned her thick and shining fall of hair, felt it slither down her back like a caressing hand on the glowing skin, bared by her clinging white jersey dress.

She was filled with a longing so acute, so fierce, it was a physical pain. She caught her breath on a strangled sob and dropped her arms, leaning her forehead against the pillar, deep in imaginings which were not to be borne, and from which she turned to flee, as if by running she could escape them, only to run straight into Luís de Capdevila.

He had been sitting deep in a cane chair at the back of the verandah, in the shadows, and rose in one fluid motion of effortless grace and peak physical condition just as she whirled to run and she ran straight into him.

The shock was too much; it was he she had been imagining and she realized he must have seen it all. The wild-rose colour ran up her face and throat then ebbed again, leaving her wide-eyed and strung up like a tautly pulled bow. A pulse beat rapidly in the faint hollow of her throat and she was in a highly volatile state. Galatea had come to life.

He was in the formal black and white of dinner jacket and frilled shirt; he had obviously been dining somewhere —with some woman, perhaps? Was that why he had not come to the *Fiesta*? He looked very handsome; hard, suffocatingly masculine, infinitely attractive.

In electric silence they stood facing each other; her hands resting lightly against his ruffled shirt as if in protest at his sudden invasion of her private dream; his hands had gone out instinctively and held her waist; the current hummed between them, a sensual awareness that was magnified to an extent that they were not aware of anything but each other.

She of his height and darkness and maleness; of the

sharp, clean scent of him; the feel of his hands on her waist; he of the splendid young body under his hands through the thin, clinging dress; of her warmth and fragrance; of the silken sheen of lipstick on the passionate mouth with the little pulse beating frantically in one corner.

Both were skidding at uncontrollable speed down the slippery slope of sexual excitement and an involuntary shiver ran through her so that her body trembled under his hands, her breath catching harshly, her eyes caught and held by the mesmerizing quality of his.

As he felt her body tremble under his hands his own breath caught and then in one swift movement of suppressed violence he had her in his arms and was kissing her with a passion and desire that brought forth from her an instinctive and equally passionate response, her mouth opening under his, her arms going up and round his neck, her body pressed against him in a way that was electrifying, rousing him still further to a pitch of hunger that rendered him deaf and blind to everything but the feel of that sweetly and terrifyingly passionate mouth under his, the softness and roundness and firmness of her body, the taste and fragrance of her skin as his mouth moved across it.

His arms tightened as his mouth moved across her face, down her throat, over her bare shoulders, leaving a trail of fire down her breast. She unbuttoned his jacket so that she could put her arms tight around the warmth and strength of his body, murmuring his name over and over; drunk with him, filled with him, brought alive by him, unable to get enough of him, wantonly yet innocently greedy for him, conscious only that this was what she had been wanting and that it was all—even more—as she had imagined. This was what had kept her awake at night; this mouth moving against hers, this hard body tight against hers, these long fingers caressing her, this dark voice telling her things in a thick, impassioned voice in his own language, things she had longed to hear.

All the pent-up emotion she had contained with such difficulty for so long burst its weakened dam, deluging her in a torrent of passionate sensuality that swept her along on its crest so that all she could do was hold tightly to him to keep from drowning.

He was as emotionally and turbulently tossed as she was, kissing her deeply and disturbingly and lingeringly, his hands tracing the curves of her body so that she arched against him convulsively, shiveringly, meltingly, blending into him, giving of herself utterly and completely.

So lost was she, so totally and completely involved in him, that when suddenly, abruptly, almost violently, he put her away from him, holding her wrists locked in his hands with cruel strength, she could only stand there, not understanding what he was doing; what had gone wrong.

She blinked at him dazedly, confusedly, shocked and bereft. 'Luís . . . ?'

He took a deep breath. His face was taut and strained and his eyes brilliant.

'You have an effect on a man that has to be experienced to be believed,' he said harshly. 'I will not apologize for actions that were pure instinct—on both our parts, but although we crossed the boundary some time ago there is much more dangerous territory ahead and you are an employee, a guest in this house, and there are rules about that sort of thing, my lovely Galatea.'

She stared at him in puzzlement. Was he accusing her of leading him on?

'I'm sorry,' she faltered uncertainly.

'*You* are sorry,' he said sardonically.

'I can't do anything right with you, can I?' Her voice was desolate.

'Oh, no,' he said mockingly. 'Not you, my beautiful amazon. Everything you do only confirms how right you are—how exactly right. You are much too dangerous for me. I am not used to such overwhelming rightness; you were way ahead of me from the start.'

'Which is what you hate, isn't it? You just can't stand the way I am,' she said miserably.

'No. I can't,' he said deliberately.

She recoiled as if he had struck her.

'Then why did you kiss me like that?' she flung at him wildly.

'I too, do things because they suit me,' he said softly.

Her mouth trembled. She could not cope with this sudden *volte face*. His words did not go with the kisses. Something had gone badly wrong.

'You obviously don't want me here,' she told him unsteadily. 'It would be better if I left.'

'What! When my sister-in-law tells me you are a tower of strength; when the children do nothing but sing your praises; when Jorge's English has improved out of all recognition—even if his frustrations have taken a turn for the worse.'

Her face flamed. He had seen them! He must think her anybody's.

'No; a thousand times no!' he said strongly. 'I cannot let you go.'

'But you must see I can't stay here—not now,' she said desperately.

'You are not going to stay here. I only came to tell you that all is ready at Cañas. The rest of the summer is always

spent there. You all leave tomorrow.'
'But not you?'
'Not I.'
'I see,' she said, though her eyes were blinded by tears.
'I am sure you will agree it is better we do not—meet—too often. It will not do, will it? Once you are at Cañas it will be easier. I shall be in Madrid.'
'You are still prepared to trust me with Jorge and the children,' she said bitterly.
'Ah,' he said expressionlessly. 'But it is not you I do not trust.'
She stared at him, unable to think clearly, emotionally distraught.
'I don't understand you,' she said at last, fretfully.
He raised his eyebrows. 'Good heavens!' he said mockingly. 'Are you telling me there is something you cannot do?'
She eyed him smoulderingly. It always came back to this. Always.
'Never,' she said between her teeth.
He smiled at her and there was something in his smile that made her heart leap in her breast.
'That's my girl,' he said softly, and in English.
She choked back a sob. 'Never!' she said again, this time vehemently. 'You may remember I told you I was a quick learner? Well, there is something else you should know. I never make the same mistake twice! Good night and goodbye, Señor de Capdevila.' She swept by him like a queen. The only thing was, she could hear him laughing.

THREE

The house at Cañas was very different from the small white house at Cabo de los Angeles. It was big, rambling, standing on the rim of a valley, the terrace built out of the living rock, looking out over the valley, which was where they grew the grapes that were marketed for the table, not for wine; the vineyards were in the north. At Cañas they also grew fruit—oranges, apricots, peaches, lemons. There were large fields of tomatoes, some of sweet corn, and a few acres of olives. Down at the end of the valley was the village of Cañas; one street and two dozen houses. The nearest real village—with shops—was five miles away, the nearest town fifteen. Cañas was isolated, but totally self-sufficient.

Water came from artesian wells sunk centuries before; bread was baked in the village and sent up to the house daily; cattle were kept for meat and milk; chickens for eggs. A generator supplied the electricity. There was a fleet of jeeps and a Land Rover in the big garages, and a stable full of horses. A wide road led straight through the centre of the valley from the village, through the vines, to where the mountain blocked its way; it then wound its way up the mountain to the house. If you liked—or had the energy, you could climb the flight of steps cut out of the mountain which ended on the terrace.

This house was also white; built of the local stone and whitewashed over. It was shaded with vines and covered in vivid bougainvillea and wistaria; all the windows had the traditional iron grilles and the front door was a massive piece of carved oak. The terrace was flat squares of pebbled granite with a low fieldstone wall at the edge, to stop you falling down the mountain.

Inside the house, floors were tiled or polished parquet; the furniture was all authentically Spanish and very old; heavy and carved or upholstered in silk and brocade with deep cushions and matching footstools. Around the large, high central hall ran a balcony that led off to the wings of the house. Over the years, bits and pieces had been added on so that passages and rooms turned up unexpectedly. The house had an atmosphere; old, solid, comforting, endurable.

Jane had a room overlooking the terrace and the valley. Her bed was high and carved with representations of the four apostles. Sheer voile curtains hung at the windows along with heavy wooden *persianas*, or venetian blinds. The floor was tiled; cool to bare feet, and she had her own bathroom and shower adjoining.

Out at the back of the house lay the tennis courts, a croquet lawn, the stables and the garages. Within five minutes walk was a modern swimming pool; but five minutes away by jeep was the original swimming pool, a circle of white marble with a vine covered pergola and marble benches and statuary, enclosed by woods of pine and cork and eucalyptus, fragrant and cool. This was the place Jane came to love best.

The first two weeks, though were desolate. She was rocked to her foundations by the discovery of her deep, rich vein of sensuality. Luís de Capdevila had found a bonanza. Night after night she relived his kisses, the scent of him, the feel of him. Day after day she woke up with him on her mind. How strange, she thought, to hate a man's ideas but love his face and his voice and his body. It was all purely physical, she told herself firmly. They were antagonists really; from different ends of the spectrum. While she desired him physically she abhorred him mentally. He was a typical, arrogant, over-confident, smooth-talking Spaniard. And she longed for him with a longing that grew instead of fading as it should.

She knew he telephoned the Señora. She eavesdropped shamelessly. But while the Señora reported on Jorge's progress, or the children's activities, or the happenings at the *finca*—and this seemed to be the major topic of conversation, there was never any mention of 'when you come down'. But though Luís was not coming, someone else was. A certain Queta dos Santos, who seemed to be a particular friend of Luís.

But the weather was glorious and Cañas was enchanting, so Jane swam in the pool, played fast and fierce tennis with Jorge, rode around the estate with the children, watched the work of the *finca*, talked with Mariáno, the foreman, about growing grapes for the table, wandered about the packing sheds and the warehouses and in and out of the village; went for long walks over the mountain and, on the Saturday two weeks after their arrival went to a wedding in the lovely little chapel that had been specially built, as had the marble swimming pool, by Luís's great-grandfather.

One of the maids, Maria-Paz Sanchez, was marrying one of the estate workers, Rafael Moréno, and the *finca* was putting on a great show.

Jane helped the Señora to decorate the chapel with flowers; lilies, carnations, gentians, red-hot pokers, lilac and purple bourgainvillea. She had never been to a

Spanish wedding before and she looked forward to it, though with a certain amount of wistful envy.

The ceremony was at five o'clock. Only a brief siesta that day. The bride was to walk to the chapel with her father, followed by the entire population of the *pueblo*, and accompanied by a violinist and a guitarist playing love-songs. As she changed into a pretty dress Jane could hear them coming, the music drifting up the valley on the warm, still air and through her open window. She also heard a car drive up. Probably the priest.

It was not until she went into the hall to join the Señora and the children that she realized they had visitors. A slender brunette with a lovely figure, wearing what Jane recognized with a pang as a Chanel suit in heavy ribbed silk the colour of pink carnations, the national flower of Spain. She was as vivid as the flower; dark brown hair, clotted cream skin, oloroso eyes. With her was a man, about Jane's age, who turned admiring eyes on her as the Señora introduced them.

'Ah, Miss Jane, come and meet some old friends of ours. Queta—this is our Miss Jane, who has been such a comfort to me this summer. Señorita Queta dos Santos, Señor Alejandro dos Santos.'

'*Encantada* . . .' breathed Alejandro, his eyes taking in the tan, the skin, the hair, the legs. 'Now I see why Jorge has tucked himself away down here for so long without complaining. I would have done the same myself.'

His sister was not quite so approving. Her narrowed eyes took in every last detail. 'So tall . . .' she murmured pityingly. 'I am quite dwarfed. And so brown.' She smoothed her own magnolia creaminess. 'I cannot stand the sun . . . I burn so easily.'

She turned away and Jane was dismissed. But not by Alejandro.

Jorge found, when he joined them, that his position had been strongly attacked and that counter-measures were immediately called for. Alejandro was a friend ... but this was love, and therefore war.

The wedding service was elaborate; a full nuptial mass that went on for a long time. The bride was tiny, not much more than five feet, and rosily plump in her white dress and veil, which she had made herself. The bridegroom was stocky and square; obviously uncomfortable in a new suit and a collar that had suddenly become too tight. But finally, they turned to face a congratulatory congregation and the procession was formed to walk back to the reception, headed by the musicians, followed by the bride and groom, the respective parents and families and then the long crocodile of guests. One of the big barns had been cleared, and there the food and wine were spread out. There were speeches, and many toasts, lots of wine and sticky, sweet things to eat. As the evening began to fade into the night, clusters of brightly-coloured paper lamps were lit and the local band began to assemble for the dancing, but before the general festivities could begin the newly-weds' new house had to be inspected.

Everything was shown; the hand-embroidered sheets, the pots, the pans, the dishes, the furniture made by the groom, especially the carved wooden cradle which caused much blushing on the part of the bride; the vast double bed made up ready and waiting, at which point there were more jokes and more blushes.

Then, leaving the happy couple to their wedding night everyone else went back to celebrate.

Jane was never able to sit down; every man in the village wanted to dance with her—*La Inglesa Rubia*; many of them wanted to touch her hair but were too polite to say so and only stared instead. So she took it out of its pins, to a general murmur of ¡*Qué guapa!* and ¡*qué color mas maravilloso!* and ¡*qué raro!* 'How pretty', 'what a marvellous colour' and 'how strange'.

'You look like a Viking queen,' Alejandro murmured, holding her a little too close as they danced, Jorge glowering from the sidelines.

'Then be warned that any misbehaviour will result in instant execution,' she told him lightly.

'I am already in danger from Jorge,' he pleaded, 'but as he had you to himself for almost three months he really has no right to complain. And what was Luís doing to keep you hidden away down here without a word? He never so much as mentioned you when he dined with us the other night.'

'How is Señor Luís?' Jane asked casually.

'As always,' shrugged Alejandro. 'A law unto himself.'

Which described him perfectly, Jane thought; which was why he found it so easy to imprison me—

As if he had read her mind: 'Which makes it difficult for Queta to put him behind her particular set of bars,' said Alejandro dryly.

'Your sister?'

'Oh, yes; she has been trying for years to bring him up to scratch. It is a more or less understood thing, of course, and it will no doubt happen in the end but Queta is becoming impatient.'

'They are *novios*?' Jane was surprised at how normal her voice sounded.

'Not officially; no ring . . . but, as I say, it has been an understood thing for ages now and everyone expects they will eventually marry; sooner if Queta has her way; later probably, because Luís usually has his.'

Jane danced on blindly, not hearing the music, not conscious of anything but what Alejandro had said. In

Spain, one's word was as good as one's engagement ring; if everyone understood you were promised then, to all intents and purposes that promise was binding. So that was the dangerous territory he had spoken of. He was already committed to someone else. No wonder he had put her away from him so forcefully. She was a temptation to which he would not allow himself to yield. Oh, yes, that was Luís de Capdevila all right. He kept to the rules; which was probably why he disapproved of Jane: she was busily working her way through the book breaking every one of them!

Suddenly the pleasure had gone out of the evening leaving her flat and dispirited. She wanted to be away from all this music and jollity; to be alone. Searching out the Señora she asked for permission to leave the festivities and go back to the house, pleading a headache, which she found she had anyway; probably as a consequence of the heartache which had come on first.

'But of course . . . Jorge or Alex will drive you back.'

'No! Please . . . I don't wish to spoil their evening. Let me just slip away. I will be all right.'

'They will be very disappointed,' warned the Señora, then she dimpled.

'They are like two dogs fighting over a juicy bone.'

Jane smiled wanly.

'Go along,' urged the Señora compassionately, thinking Miss Jane did look strained. 'I will—how you say—cover for you.'

Once outside in the sweet warmth of the fruit-scented air Jane did not want to drive back. She wanted to wander, slowly and meditively.

She had to come to terms with this new knowledge and add it to the store she was accumulating about herself; especially the most vital piece of all: that she was in love, for better or worse and probably worse, with Luís de Capdevila.

Jane had never been in love before. She had had boy friends and one or two of them had talked of love but none of them had reached her. Her feelings had lain dormant. Now they were clamorously alive; wanting, demanding, longing. And she could not have. No wonder he had talked of dangerous territory, she thought, not for a moment realizing that she herself, her suddenly come-alive beauty, her awakening sensuality, was that very territory.

Love was painful, she decided. It was not moonlight and roses; it was not sweet nothings and a glow of romance over everything. It was confusion, and an aching longing and a jealousy that burned hot and fierce. It was a disturbing excitement that made one look forward to the coming day; it was feeling alive, down to toe- and finger-nails, and wanting to be with the one you loved; to feel the sense of safety and belonging, of security, that it gave. It was committing oneself to another human being heart and soul, as she had to Luís de Capdevila.

Only he had not done so to her. Oh, she knew he was attracted to her. She was not stupid. Any woman worthy of the name knew when a man found her desirable. Luís's kisses had told her that; she knew she had given him a deep and unforgettable pleasure, perhaps the greatest any woman had ever given him, but that was all purely physical. Of the rest of her he disapproved. And Jane was not the type of girl to pretend to be what she was not; she was too honest. In any case, she had no desire to entrap a man by pretending to be what she was not; if he was that much of a fool she did not want him anyway.

Luís was no fool; he had a keen mind, a profound intelligence and a marked sense of humour. He and Jane had sparked off a chain reaction in each other, but whereas Jane's had got out of control and exploded, leaving her fragmented and confused, his was tightly controlled, like the man himself.

What on earth did he see in Queta dos Santos? She was beautiful, but Jane knew with an infallible instinct that beauty was not enough for Luís. He appreciated it—he was a Spaniard—but if that was all there was it would not be enough. What a woman *was*; that was important to Luís. What she stood for; how she thought. Was she understanding, compassionate, loving? Jane knew this. And to her, Queta possessed none of those qualities. Yet that same, infallible instinct told Jane that Luís had discovered—and appreciated—in her, some of them. Had he not said she had *sal*? Why, then, *why* had he gone behind that impenetrable wall of Spanish formality? Had he over-reached himself? Had he not meant to give into his obvious attraction? Had she led him on?

Questions swimming round in her brain like fish fruitlessly circling a goldfish bowl she walked on, deep in endless speculation and conjecture. Jane was a thinking girl; there had to be a reason for everything. All she had to do was find it.

It was quiet and peaceful once she had left the noise of the fiesta behind. In the bright starlight the white road through the valley was bleached and bare; the fruit trees on either side of it dark and laden, almost ready for harvest. The air was still and heavy; August in the valley was very hot, with temperatures well over one hundred degrees day after day. The sound of Jane's sandals was hardly noticeable; the only noise was her own steady breathing, the repeated hooting of an owl, and the muted cries of the bats in the fruit trees. The air was deeply scented with the mouth-watering fruitiness of peaches and apricots and nectarines and plums; with the richness of wild figs and with the grapes.

Ahead of her, up on the rim of the valley, the house waited, the terrace lamps lit and beckoning. Luís de Capdevila's house.

They had both been caught up in a special kind of magic, she decided, only he had got through the net; she had been so inextricably tangled that only his hands could set her free. Whatever happened, though, he would never forget her. She was sure of that. She had felt him tremble as he kissed her, sensed the raging fires that were on the edge of becoming out of control. This sent her into a reverie of what he would be like as a lover, and so lost was she in this that her feet had carried her up the road and half-way up the flight of steps before she realized it. It was then that a sudden prickle at the back of her neck told her she was being watched. There was something, or someone in the thick scrub of the mountain, amongst the pines and eucalyptus, and it—or they—were watching her. Her senses crawled at the knowledge. She did not stop, but continued climbing the steps, though she quickened her pace slightly, taking the occasional double step.

She felt her scalp crawl. There were no wild animals in the valley apart from small ones; foxes, rabbits, hares. If it had been the dogs they would have come to her; she had made friends with them. Curro, the big golden labrador and Tina, the Señora's half-blind spaniel. No, it was not the dogs. But it was something. Listening hard, hardly breathing, she could hear nothing but she could *sense* it, *feel* it. Could it be Jorge, playing a trick? Or he and Alejandro, annoyed with her for leaving them? Had they come up by way of the fruit groves, climbed up the mountain and waited to spring out at her crying 'Boo!'?

She was more than half-way up now; she could see the iron grille work on the windows; see the pools of light spread by the lamps, which burned all night. Suddenly, a twig snapped. There *was* something there. Like a hare she took to her heels, leaping the steps two and three at a time. Thank God the heavy, studded front door was never locked. She burst through it like an Olympic champion, slamming it behind her, leaning against it breathing hard, feeling her heart banging away at her rib-cage.

'*¿Señorita?*' It was Pepe, the old major-domo.

'*¡Hola!* Pépe. *Buenas noches.*'

'You have climbed the steps too fast, Señorita. It is a long climb and should be taken slowly, even with long legs such as yours.'

'You are right, Pépe. I ran the last two flights because I was startled by a noise in the woods—a rabbit, perhaps, or a fox?'

'There are hedgehogs at night,' he said doubtfully. 'They hunt for food in the dark, but I do not think they will want to eat you, Señorita.'

She smiled dutifully. 'You are right, Pépe. I have come home early as I am tired. The others will be along later. Good night, Pepe.'

FOUR

Had Queta dos Santos not been all-but officially engaged to Luís de Capdevila Jane would still not have liked her. There was a shallowness, a lack of depth, a hardness just beneath the soft-surface. It was not Luís who held her main interest; it was what he possessed. It was Capdevila S.A., the *fincas*, the *fabricas*, the bank—for that was the main source of the family's wealth. They were what interested Queta, whose conversation was always about things; furs, jewellery, cars, a private areoplane, which Jane gathered she was pressing Luís to buy so that they could be at Cañas in less than half the time it took to drive.

She and Luís would make a handsome couple; of that there was no doubt. Her feline femininity would set off and be set off by his masculinity. She was very lovely, of course, and always beautifully turned out. Not for Queta the hot and drying sun; she protected her skin by shady trees and a big hat; she did not play tennis and glow, like Jane; she rode, but not far and never jumped. While the others held impromptu jump-offs she rode a sedate, well-behaved mare and was as immaculate when she returned as when she set off; Jane came back tousled and wind-blown, in a casual shirt and jeans, for all the world like some cow-girl. Nor did she swim. She sat by the pool in a cunningly designed, beautifully cut bikini and shuddered distastefully at Jane, in a navy-blue plain nylon Speedo, doing double somersaults and backward corkscrews from the highest board at the modern pool, or jumping from the marble benches at the old pool, all accompanied by splashing and shouting and cries of 'Show me, Miss Jane' from the children.

'These English girls are so hearty,' she complained wincingly to the Señora.

'Luís calls her an Amazon,' smiled the Señora indulgently.

'Does he indeed! I suppose she is like some warrior . . .'

'A very clever one,' said the Señora dryly. 'A Double First at Oxford.'

'She will need brains,' Queta said cruelly. 'She has nothing else that will be of any use.'

'Miss Jane has many qualities,' said the Señora icily. 'She is kind, and loving and absolutely trustworthy; she has the courage of a lion and the gaiety of a lark; she never complains and she is game for anything. We all love her very much.'

'I find her very overpowering,' shrugged Queta. 'So big . . . she quite overlooks Alejandro . . .'

'He is doing his best to counteract that,' said the Señora dryly.

'A boy,' Queta dismissed him. 'A man would have different ideas; Luís, for instance . . .'

The Señora thought of the way she had seen Luís watching Jane when she was not aware, and wondered. Her brother-in-law was an interior man, he did not reveal much of himself, but he was an immensely comforting one and in the two years since her husband's death he had been her refuge and her strength. Carlos had adored and been adored by his wife; they had been ideally happy until the senseless car crash that killed him. That was why Luís had been angry about the Lamborghini; it was on that very road that Carlos had died. But Luís was a fair-minded man; once he knew that Jane had been properly taught—which in fact he had seen really, as he watched her take the Lamborghini away from them—he had ceased to protest.

Queta had obviously been thinking about Luís too.

'When shall we see Luís?' she asked idly.

'He will be here for the twins' birthday; that is one occasion he never misses.'

'But that is almost a week away . . .'

'He has much to do, and he did spend rather a lot of time with us at Cabo de los Angeles.'

Queta let that one pass.

'And it will be harvesting time soon; he is always here for that,' said the Señora comfortably.

The twins' birthday at Cañas was always an occasion for a big celebration, to which all the children of the *finca* were invited. Simona, the cook, always baked a big sponge cake which she iced, and the Señora hired a conjuror or a Punch and Judy show.

Over breakfast the twins opened their presents. The Señora had given Luisíto a beautiful microscope with which to study his marine flora and fauna; Inés received a beautiful gold watch with a delicate filigree strap—'just like *Mamacíta's*' she crowed.

Jane had sent to England for Luisíto's present; a beautifully illustrated book on Marine Biology, which rendered him awed and speechless with delight and for which he almost hugged Jane to death. For Inés, she produced a personally signed photograph of the pop star who was her idol. Jane's brother knew him because he was an amateur racing driver.

'Does he really know him, to speak to and to touch?' Inés asked in hushed tones.

'Yes, truly he does.'

'And this is his real, own handwriting, that says "To my dear friend and loyal fan Inés Dolores María del Carmen de Capdevila y Ayalá?"'

'Cross my heart and hope to die,' swore Jane solemnly.

'I will sleep with it under my pillow,' Inés swore fervently. 'And perhaps when I come to England your brother will introduce me to him?'

'I will see to it that he does,' promised Jane.

After lunch the children came and the conjuror did his tricks, producing *pesetas* from ears, and doves from hats and guinea pigs from paper bags.

Then there were games, including a very enthusiastic game of blind man's buff. Jane made a very good blind man, and the children refused to let her hand over the blindfold to someone else. She was feeling her way across the terrace, arms outstretched, when suddenly she noticed a change in the babble of sound around her, a slight hush, a murmur, a rustle of whispers. They were up to something. Inés was a great deviser of strategems. Listening carefully for a voice she heard a smothered giggle: Inés. Swiftly she pounced. It was an arm, but though the voice was Inés it was not her arm. It was a man's arm in a sleeve.

'Jorge?'

More giggles from Inés. 'Wrong, Miss Jane. Try again.'

Jane felt her way up the arm to the shoulder; her fingers touched a jaw and she knew, she knew. But she said nothing, wanting to prolong the contact as long as she could. She touched a mouth, smiling—oh, how she remembered that mouth ... 'Alejandro?' she asked.

Inés shrieked with laughter. 'You will never guess, Miss Jane. Give up, give up!'

'I never give up,' Jane said clearly.

She ran her hand lightly up the face, her fingers trembling slightly over the eyes and up to the hair. She brought up her other hand and ran them both lightly over his face.

'Señor Luís,' she stated calmly.

The scarf was untied and it was he, holding it in his hands, onyx eyes amused. 'Even your fingers are educated, I see.'

'A simple matter of deduction,' she answered lightly. 'Who else around here is taller than I?'

'Liar,' he said softly, for her ears alone. Then: 'How are you Miss Jane?' he asked formally.

'I am very well, as you see,' she answered, just as formally. 'And you?'

'I too, am surviving.' Their eyes met, held, locked, until she turned away to the children who were clamouring around her.

'Yes, we will stop the game whilst you see what your Uncle Luís has brought you.'

She went across to where the food and drink were laid out and picked up a glass of champagne—provided for the adults.

'That was very clever, Miss Jane.' She looked down into the cream-sherry eyes of Queta dos Santos.

'I have been very well educated,' she said modestly.

'Even down to the feel of Señor Luís?'

'Simple deduction,' protested Jane airily, gulping champagne.

A conflagration of jealousy burned away behind Queta's eyes.

'A detective too?' she purred dangerously.

I could detect Luís de Capdevila bound, gagged and blindfolded, thought Jane, hoping desperately Luís would be staying, wishing desperately he had not come. She gulped more champagne. Perhaps if she drowned her sorrows . . .

'Miss Jane, come. We are going to see Uncle Luís's present,' said Inés, pulling at Jane's hand.

'Yes, of course,' said Jane, draining her champagne glass. 'To hear is to obey.'

'You could have fooled me.' Luís de Capdevila stood just by Inés.

Jane cast him one speaking glance. 'That'll be the day,' she said feelingly, and followed Inés.

Dammit, he was always throwing her into a state of confusion.

She wished she could get drunk on champagne and wash him out of her system. But look what had happened after all that Sangría! The thought put wings on her heels and she fairly flew after Inés, who was running at full pelt in the direction of the stables, closely followed by Luisíto.

'Where is the surprise, where?' she demanded, coming to a full stop in the yard and seeing nothing.

'Come with me and find out,' said her Uncle, coming up on her.

'Is it one each or one for both of us,' asked Luisíto practically.

'Follow me and you will find out.'

'Said the Pied Piper,' murmured Jane and flinched at the look he gave her. The sheer churning excitement he generated was in full cry; his presence more intoxicating than a magnum of champagne.

He led the children over to one of the stables. 'Wait there,' he ordered, and disappeared inside.

They waited, hopping from one foot to another in excitement and anticipation. Then Luís appeared, leading on either side of him two beautiful Palomino ponies. The children went mad. They hurled themselves at Luís, hugging his legs, his arms, anything they could get hold of. Then they fell on the ponies, while Luís and their mother, Queta, Jorge and Alejandro, who had all followed behind, looked on. Jorge and Alejandro had taken up their usual positions either side of Jane and Luís raised his eyebrows at her. When she went over to stroke the ponies he said sotto voce: 'Your bodyguard?'

She gave him a smile of honeyed sweetness. 'Safety in numbers,' she said.

With a laugh she felt in her toes he let her go forward to the ponies; golden and alert in the sunlight.

'Oh, you beauties,' she said lovingly. 'You two beautiful things.'

And what a present, she thought. Not one but *two* pure-bred ponies. No wonder Queta is so eager to get her first cheque book. She put a hand onto an arching, silken-maned neck, and a soft mouth nuzzled her cheek.

'Even the horses,' marvelled a dark voice. 'Is there no end to your conquests?'

She looked into those brilliant eyes. 'My middle name is Ghengis Khan,' she said demurely, and she felt that laugh again.

'May we ride, may we ride?' clamoured the twins.

'You have guests still,' he reminded them. 'But we will all ride tomorrow morning—early. Seven o'clock.' He looked at Jane as he spoke.

Her eyes were sparkling, great pools of chartreuse, clear and alive with mischief. '*Se obedecé pero no se cúmple*,' she said innocently. 'We accept the order but we do not carry it out' and left him laughing.

On horseback, as she had known he would be, Luís de Capdevila was tremendous. *Mucho,* thought Jane with a sigh, using the Spanish word because it said it all. ¡*Mucho!* He rode a powerful, raking chestnut, aptly named, full of strength and high-bred nervousness, which Jane eyed longingly from her own sandy colt.

'No—not this one.' The voice was quite definite and the threat was as strong as the feel of his hand on her wrist. 'You are a strong girl, my beautiful Amazon, and you ride like a dream but there are things beyond even you. I have given orders.'

She met the implacable but urbane black eyes mutinously.

'I told you once before,' he went on as if he had not noticed, 'around here I pay the piper—'

'And play him too,' she flashed.

'—therefore I call the tune.'

'Yes, maestro,' she said with an edge to her sarcasm with which he could have shaved, but at the answering gleam in his eyes she spurred her colt in fright and was away, feeling the horse respond, taking the stone wall like a leaf blown in the wind, leaving Jorge and Alejandro, her constant shadows, milling round in shocked surprise before they could gather themselves and their horses together and come after her, the twins with them, leaving Luís to accompany Queta, who never galloped.

The woods were cool, smelling of pine and eucalyptus, dappled with sunlight and sweet with birdsong. The horses feet thudded thickly on the soft earth as they picked their way down the mountain to the floor of the valley and away into open country, where Jane urged the colt again into an easy, almost flying rhythm. Ahead were the first walls, and the colt wafted over them like a feather.

He was a beautiful animal, young and full of spirit, like Jane. Together they made an unforgettable sight as they ran the course of the dried river bed, climbed the bank and sailed over the wall behind it. The air sang past her, whipping her hair, in a silken tail like her horse, flapping the collar of her open shirt. As they came to the woods again Jane let him slow, snorting and prancing, blowing down his nose, thoroughly enjoying himself.

'You are a gorgeous thing and I love you,' Jane told him, patting the arched neck. His ears pricked knowingly.

'I am jealous,' said Luís, coming up behind her on the stallion.

'You have the most maddening habit of stealing up on people,' Jane told him crossly, feeling her colour rise, 'even on a horse!'

Why was he taunting her so and where was Queta?

'I think you have mislaid something,' she told him.

He smiled into her eyes. 'I don't think so; you are here.'

'I mean your fiancée,' Jane said pink-cheeked.

'I never mislay fiancées,' he assured her solemnly.

She turned her head to hide her smile, and the horses walked on companionably, bridles clinking, leather creaking.

'I could ride him, you know,' Jane said suddenly, challengingly. 'I have strong wrists.'

'But mine are stronger,' he said flatly. 'Do not disobey me in this.' He cracked the whip. 'Rebellion must have a goal. Riding *Castaña* would prove only that you are rebellious.'

'I am *not* rebellious,' she told him from between clenched teeth. 'I only do what I am capable of doing and I *know* I could ride him, but if you find me rebellious it is because you make me so; you and your damned assumptions. I am not usually like this,' she told him wildly. 'You have the strangest effect on me . . .'

'Go on,' he invited softly.

'No,' she said curtly. He had enough on her as it was. She was damned if she was going to give him any more leverage. And why was he so blatantly seeking her company when he had told her—so definitely—that night at the Cape that it would be better if they did not meet too often? Admittedly it was hard not to; he was the twins' guardian, this was his estate. But he did not *have* to seek her out. It really was too bad of him when he knew the effect he had on her. But what if she had the same effect on him? What if he too had come to love the verbal battles, the constant challenge, the sharp sound of clashing swords. They did not do each other any real injury . . . except to my heart, thought Jane with a pang. I can't tell if I have managed to wound his; he does not look as though he is bleeding . . .

The sound of horses rapidly approaching from behind heralded Queta, not at all happy at the tete-a-tete between Luís and Jane. The dark-gold eyes threw daggers at Jane while she edged her horse between the chestnut and the sandy colt. Without a word, Jane dropped back and at once Jorge and Alejandro took up position and began to wrangle as to who had the prior claim on Jane; Jorge with his invitation to a *tienta* of young calves at a neighbouring ranch; Alejandro with his invitation to a tennis party.

The twins backed Jorge; they wanted to go and see the bulls themselves.

'They are only calves, Miss Jane, about ten months

old,' explained Inés importantly, 'and they have to be tested to see if they are brave. It is very interesting. They don't kill them,' she said kindly, 'not like in the ring. Jorge has a go, don't you Jorge?'

Jorge shrugged. 'Sometimes.' He was not feeling very happy. It was bad enough to have to contend with Alejandro trying to move in on Jane; now here was his *Tío* Luís outrunning them all on that brute of a stallion, in blatant and obvious pursuit of the summer-long object of Jorge's unrequited passion. Time was of the essence; the summer two-thirds gone, and she had blocked every effort he'd made so far to make love to her. He had his reputation to think of after all! Things were beginning to be desperate. Every chance must be seized. Perhaps if he could impress her with his prowess with the bulls ... He had not thought this English *rubia* would be so hard to pin down, or that he would be prepared to devote *a whole summer* to her pursuit. She was so splendid, of course. Game for anything—up to and stopping short of allowing him to make love to her. She swam, rode, water-skied, played tennis, all with great skill and enjoyment. She was a great person to be with even if she was the keenest competition. As Alejandro had discovered when she beat him hollow at what he was unbeatable at; a hard, fast game of tennis. The only consolation to Jorge was that Alejandro was not getting anywhere either. She held them both off with those long arms that matched those marvellous legs.

Jorge fell back to let the twins come up, and stayed behind Jane so he could watch her, dreaming about what he would like to do, when a hard voice said:

'Do not waste your time there, *chico*. Miss Jane is not for the likes of you.'

Jorge came to with a start to find his Uncle eyeing him with a look that said he had seen and understood all. Jorge had the grace to blush.

'The summer is not over yet,' he shrugged.

'You could pursue her all winter too and still not succeed. It will take a particular hunter to capture that particular specimen.'

'She is a woman,' Jorge said smugly, 'and women like to be captured.'

'Not that one. Cage her and she'll die. She is totally liberated, remember?'

Jorge looked at his uncle sharply.

'You have seen a very great deal in a short time,' he observed frostily. 'Allow me to point out that I have spent more time with her than you and I know her somewhat better.'

'Do you indeed!' The dark eyes measured him dispassionately.

Jorge flushed again. 'Not that way—though I have been trying to all summer.'

'I told you,' Luís de Capdevila said laconically. 'An Amazon.'

Jorge sighed. 'She is splendid, isn't she? So good at so many things... She makes me feel...'

'Inadequate?'

Jorge looked at his uncle. 'Why, yes! How did you know?'

'She has that effect on people.' His Uncle stared broodingly at the straight-backed figure ahead, chatting amiably to the twins.

'I hope there are lots like her at Oxford,' gloated Jorge. 'Jane says there are.'

'I doubt it,' his uncle said abruptly. 'Jane is unique.'

'But they have passed a law at Parliament in England which says men and women are now absolutely equal,' said Jorge.

'Only in law,' his uncle said flatly.

'So there will plenty of opportunity for women to be like Jane, if they wish. Jane says this is what counts: not that a woman *will* someday be Prime Minister of England, but that she can be *if she wishes*. Jane says that women are no longer restricted to their purely biological role, which has confined them to only one role in life for so many centuries. Now they are recognized as human beings who happen to be of the female sex and there is nothing they cannot do.'

'Is this what she has been teaching you?' the dark voice asked grimly.

'Oh, no; she teaches me nothing but English, but we talk a lot and we have talked many times of this.'

'She truly believes, then, in this thing of Women's Liberation?' asked Luís de Capdevila slowly.

'Oh, yes,' said Jorge carelessly. 'Not militantly, but fervently. She says that women do not have to be equal if they do not *wish* to; passing a law cannot make this so, but for those who wish to be treated as a human being first and a woman second, instead of the other way round, well then it is a very good thing.'

'And does she see herself that way?'

Jorge laughed shortly. 'Yes, *she* does. I see it the other way. So does Alejandro. What one sees when one sees Jane is a woman who is also a human being.'

Luís mouth twitched. 'Indeed,' he said, as if saying 'Amen'.

'And marriage and children?' Luís asked after a moment. 'Does she not want them?'

'If she finds she does then she will have them; that is what she says.'

Luís's laugh was savage. 'Man proposes, woman disposes,' he said viciously, and spurred the stallion on to where Jane was riding along lost in thought.

'You look like Alice in Wonderland with that hair down your back,' he said.

'I am,' Jane said dreamily, not yet fully conscious of him. 'Spain is wonderland to me.'

'You like my country.' Something in the way he said it brought Jane fully back to her surroundings and to him. The rose colour stained her face and throat. 'I always have,' she said rather breathlessly. Then, artlessly: 'Ever since the first time I came here. It spoke to me.'

'Saying what?'

'Oh ... that here was a way of life, a culture, a civilization very different from my own but with much to offer. I liked the food, climate, the music, the language ...'

'And Spaniards?'

She was careful not to meet those gleaming eyes. 'Naturally,' she said lightly.

'But surely you were warned about us?' he probed.

She felt her heart begin to thud. 'Oh, yes. From the very beginning. *Cuidádo con los hombres españoles*, they told me. "Beware of Spanish men".'

'We do have a—certain reputation,' he agreed suavely.

'Well merited,' said Jane feelingly, before she could stop herself.

'You have had some difficulties?' he enquired innocently.

'Hah!' said Jane darkly.

'You intrigue me,' he told her silkily. 'I would not

have thought you, with your liberated ideas, capable of being disturbed by what is, after all, an occupational hazard for women who look like you.'

Wide eyed and open mouthed she stared at him. His eyes were sparkling—no they weren't—they were *smouldering*! Instantly she looked away, staring between the colt's ears, thoroughly rattled. He was flirting with her!

She heard a smothered laugh, and outraged she turned instantly to quell him with a few well chosen words but met his eyes. A reluctant smile widened into a grin which slid into whole-throated laughter, but as she continued to hold his eyes something in them changed and her smile faded gradually as her mouth dried and she felt her heart leap in her throat.

Cuidádo con los hombres españoles. The sentence glowed brightly in her mind. She knew he wanted to kiss her; he knew she wanted him to. Of their own violition her lips parted and she swayed towards him.

'May we not all share the joke?' There was Queta again. This time she was furious. Her voice broke the spell; Jane jerked upright and the colt, taking this as a signal, gathered himself and leapt forward.

'Well, really,' she heard Queta's voice fade behind her as the colt took off, and she let him have his head, needing to escape from the shimmering mesh of the man's radiant sensuality that already had her floundering in a big way. This sort of thing could lead nowhere but to heartbreak. He was morally bound to Queta dos Santos, wasn't he? Why then play with her? Was he deliberately setting out to show her that she was only as free as he allowed her to be? That she was not liberated from her own desires and instincts?

The thud of the colt's hooves pounded out his name

as she had chanted it on the night he had kissed her.
'Luís, Luís Luís, Luís . . .'

She sobbed out loud, and set the colt at a looming stone wall and as he took it, like a bird, she screamed his name out once, despairingly, 'Luís . . .'

FIVE

Jane took care to avoid Luís de Capdevila as much as possible after that. It was not easy; she could hardly wander off on her own; but she took every opportunity to take the children with her to the pool, or for walks, or for cycle rides, for they had discovered some old bikes in one of the sheds and Jane had taught both children to ride, so well that they were now demanding new bikes for Christmas!

And it was when she was with the children; gathering wild blackberries for Simona to make into a jelly, or wandering about the estate roads or through the woods, that she had again the pricking feeling that she was being watched. The children seemed to feel nothing, and there was never anyone to be seen, but the feeling was strong and made her uneasy. Whenever Jorge or Alejandro were with them she did not feel it; it was when she was either alone or with the children. She wondered if she should tell the Señora, but decided that there was not enough to warrant worrying her. A 'feeling' was not proof. So she said nothing. Until the episode of the camera.

They had all been to the marble pool and were on their way back, when Jane realized she had left the camera behind. It was a good one, and whilst she was sure it would not be taken she did not like to leave it lying around. Besides, it had an unfinished roll of film in it which she intended to use up when they went to the engagement party that night.

So she said to the others, 'You go on; I won't be five minutes and I'll catch up with you.'

She ran back to the pool but the camera was not there. She searched thoroughly and carefully, under the benches, in the changing cabins. It had gone. Suddenly, she knew that whoever it was or whatever it was that watched her was there again. Her skin pricked and her heart quickened. She felt menaced, somehow. It was very quiet, the day fading slowly; almost six o'clock. Trying not to show any nervousness she stood up, and then as though deciding that it was no use searching further turned away to walk back to join the others, and her eye caught a fleeting glimpse of something or someone back in the trees. She had an impression of a shadow, a big one, and clearly, across the silence, came the sound of rustling bushes and a bird, startled, streaked over her head. With a smothered cry she took to her heels. She was not sure where she ran, she only knew she had to.

Coming back from the other side of the *finca* Luís de Capdevila was driving back to the house, his mind preoccupied with several things, driving automatically, when suddenly something burst out of the bushes about twenty yards ahead and streaked across the road. He braked sharply, and sat stunned. For a moment he had thought it was Jane. He closed his eyes and visualized what he had seen. It *was* Jane. Running hard and fast, long legs covering the ground, an expression of blind terror on her face. She had crossed the road and disappeared into the woods and from the direction in which she was heading she would cross the road again where it curved, further down the mountain. Re-starting the jeep he put his foot down and raced down the road. Even at the rate Jane was running he should be able to get down to where she would come out of the trees in time to stop her.

By the time he stopped the jeep and got out, running to the side of the road, he could hear her coming. She was slamming into bushes, tearing leaves, not really looking where she was going. What had happened to cause such panic? And where were the others? The children?

She burst out of the bushes, graceful as a gazelle even in her panic, not even seeing him as he moved towards her. She cannoned into him with such force that she knocked him down and they both rolled over onto the road. She let out a cry of sheer terror and would have been up and away had he not caught her by the ankle. She tried to kick him but he pulled her down again and fought her as she flailed at him with her fists. She had no idea who he was and what was happening; she was in the grip of an unreasoning terror that had whitened her face and blanked out her eyes.

'Jane,' he said sharply. 'Jane!'

She swung an arm at him, fist clenched, but he caught it, and pinned it behind her. Her other hand went for his face but he parried it and managed to pin it with the other, bringing her up hard against him. Her body was stiff.

'Jane,' he said again. 'It is Luís!' He took hold of her chin and held her face so that she had to look at him. 'Jane,' he said again, calmly. 'You are safe now. Look at me—it is Luís!'

Her breath was rasping in her throat, whistling with effort, but he felt the rigidity of her body soften and her eyes lost their blankness and registered that it was indeed him.

'Oh, Luís,' she said, and buried her face against his chest, trembling uncontrollably. He let go her wrists and put his arms around her. Her own came up to clutch at him as she held on to him tightly.

'There was someone—something—in the woods. It was watching me and I heard it; I think it came after me but I ran. I've heard it before. It watches me . . .'

He held her while her breathing slowed, sitting on the ground at the side of the road, her head under his chin, feeling the comforting steady beat of his heart under her cheek. He could feel the tension slowly leave her body and he put up a hand and stroked the leaf and branch-strewn hair, picking off bits of leaf and twig where they had been caught up in her headlong flight.

'There was something there, there was! I've felt it before. When I'm alone or with the children.'

'Where are the children?' he asked gently, alertly.

'With Jorge and Alejandro. I went back to the pool to get my camera. I left it there but when I went to look for it it had gone.' She lifted her head to look at him urgently. 'It was not there, Luís. I know I left it. Whatever—or whoever was in the trees must have taken it . . .'

She put her head back against the safe and solid warmth of his chest.

'Perhaps a tramp, or a gypsy,' he said matter-of-factly. 'They would steal your camera if they could. Did you see anything?' he asked casually.

'Just a glimpse; a shadow—something big.' She shivered. 'It watches me.'

'We all do that,' he said softly.

At once he felt the change in her body and cursed himself for a fool. She became conscious of the way he was holding her and she pushed herself away from him. He let her go. She scrambled to her feet.

'I'm sorry,' she said stiffly. 'I did not mean to hurl myself at you.' At the words she flushed scarlet.

He got lightly to his feet. 'You didn't,' he said. 'I put myself right in your way so as to stop you.'

'I panicked,' she said disgustedly.

'You were startled.'

'There *was* something there,' she said low voiced.

'There was.'

'It is not unknown for gypsies and tramps to be seen in the woods.'

'But why just watch me; why creep around so—so secretively?'

'Because they know they would be in trouble if they were caught.'

'I'm sorry,' she said miserably. 'It's just—I can't stand being watched like that. It makes me nervous.'

'I'll have the men keep an eye open. If there is anyone there we will catch him.'

'There is no "if" about it,' she said tensely. 'There is someone out there. I know it.' She turned away, smoothing back her hair nervously.

'Come on; I'll drive you back,' he said. 'We will say nothing to my sister-in-law about this; she is of a very nervous disposition and she would worry.'

He went up to her; put an arm about her shoulders. 'In future do not go about the woods on your own or with just the children. Take Jorge and Alejandro with you. I'll make sure that if there is anyone in the woods they will be caught.'

She stood with her head bent, brushing dirt and leaves from her shirt. He could see the dark crescents of her eyelashes against the gold of her skin. The arm tightened fractionally, then dropped away.

'In you get,' he said. 'I'll drive you back and you shall have the sovereign English remedy for upsets like these.'

'What's that?' she asked, in spite of herself.

He grinned at her. 'A cup of tea.'

Queta made no bones about her dislike of Jane. The kitten had claws and did not hesitate to scratch. Luís was her property; the English girl was here for the summer only and it did not do for her to get ideas above her station. Without delay Queta proceeded to demonstrate to Jane her claim—staked and registered—to be the future Señora Luís de Capdevila. Her proprietory air said a plain—'Hands off! Private Property'.

On the way to the engagment party that night at a neighbouring *finca*, where the daughter of the house was announcing it officially, Queta drove with Luís. Jane went with her usual escorts.

The party—like the house—was lavish. About two hundred guests, two bands, a discotheque and enough food and drink to feed two thousand.

Jane was in a febrile, glittery mood. She threw herself into the pool of admiration at the deep end and danced and flirted indiscriminately with a great number of admiring men. She was constantly on the dance floor, so that she had no time to brood or dwell constantly on Luís de Capdevila, though she was conscious of his presence every single second, darkly elegant this time in a white dinner jacket, reminding her with thrilling clarity of how he had acted the last time he was dressed that way. He danced; she saw him on the dance floor with Queta; with Lolita, the novia; with the Señora, with their hostess, with various other women. But he did not come near Jane.

She saw to it it that she was never in any group of which he was part; that when he was not dancing, she was, and *vice versa*. She refused to allow either Jorge or Alejandro to get her alone in the deeply shadowed corners of a lamp-lit terrace, and dealt charmingly with other predatory males who were very much taken with the so-tall, intriguingly self-confident English girl with the mass of ash blonde hair and skin like a nectarine, set off by a floating chiffon dress in swirling blues and greens which shimmered like the colours on the surface of a pool of petroleum.

But no matter where she was he was with her. She felt his presence with the back of her head, and the sound of his voice was like a jerk on the invisible thread which tied her to him. But Queta had the obvious claim. Jane overheard her being asked: 'And when can we expect a similar announcement about you and Luís?'

Queta sounded as though she had just drunk a saucerful of cream. 'Sooner than you think,' she purred.

Jane went blindly on to the dancefloor with Jorge—or was it Federico—or perhaps José—to do an enthusiastic samba, followed by a rhumba then a paso-dóble, then a tango. Never ceasing to twirl, to gyrate, to glide, to shake, but never able to free herself.

Then the music changed; the band went for a well-earned rest and the discotheque took over; lights were lowered, strobe lights began to flicker sinuously over faces and bodies, blues and greens and yellows, illuminating then shadowing; the music was soft, sinuous, with an insidious beat and a langorous rhythm. Soul music.

At once over came Alejandro. 'Ah ... at last,' he said, 'I have hardly danced with you all evening, Miss Jane.'

'Only three times,' Jane told him dryly.

'What is that? Not even three times three would be enough!'

He gathered her into his arms, as close as he could. He was an excellent dancer, holding her firmly, cheek to cheek, his hand in hers and other arm wrapped round her body. He too smelled of something fresh, not like Luís, but nice. But then all Spanish men smelled delicious; it was a combination of the cologne they all wore, and tobacco. The essence of Spain was to Jane, the way it smelled. When you stepped out of the plane it hit you; a combination of pine trees, cologne and Spanish tobacco. That particular combination had the power to transport her back to Spain no matter where she was. She closed her eyes and let herself drift on the beat and power of the music. Alejandro was not as tall as Luís but she could, with her eyes shut, use her imagination.

'You are magic, Jane,' whispered Alejandro. 'You have cast a spell on me.'

Suddenly she could bear him no longer. He was not Luís and the talk of spells only brought home to her the one in which she was held. She made to push him away.

'Please Alejandro.'

But he was not to be put off. The music and Jane in his arms had roused him too strongly. His arms tightened. Her own stiffened.

'Alejandro, please!'

She pushed him hard with her not inconsiderable strength and he let her go suddenly, so that she staggered back into someone who caught her arms, saying in tones of amused reproof: 'What, fighting them off literally, my dear Miss Jane! No wonder I have hardly been able to get to you all evening. I think it is time I danced with you myself; that will give you time to get your priorities right.'

With arrogant ease he turned her unresisting body into his arms and moved off onto the floor. She stared fixedly at his frilled shirt front and dared not melt against him as she longed to; her traitorous body would betray her and she could not stand another rebuff. But every nerve in her body was responding to his nearness; his hand on her bare skin was like a naked flame but there was no pain, only a chain reaction of exquisite pleasure.

'You have made another conquest there,' he said teasingly. 'Is there no end to them?'

'You said I had a Spanish soul,' Jane pointed out as lightly as she could, still not meeting eyes she knew would be laughing at her. 'I think perhaps I was a *conquistador* in an earlier reincarnation ...'

'Obviously; a combination of Pizárro and the great Cortés himself—liberators both,' he said sardonically.

'They did it with the sword,' Jane parried swiftly. 'I have no need of such weapons.'

'Indeed no,' he said softly. 'You have weapons of your own ...'

Her eyes flew to his; they were gleaming, a little flame flickering in their depths.

'You look very beautiful tonight,' he said, his eyes trailing over her like his fingers.

Jane's breath felt constricted. 'Thank you,' she managed to say.

'Spain has an—effect on you, obviously,' he went on.

Not Spain, she wanted to tell him; you.

'As Jorge pointed out, you have indeed—blossomed.'

'I am enjoying myself,' she said honestly.

'Now—or in general?' He was probing.

'Always,' she answered evasively.

'It is not Jorge who should enter the diplomatic service,' he commented dryly.

'I am on my best behaviour tonight,' she said sweetly.

'Is that what it is? I think I prefer the perversity to the purr ...'

She smothered a giggle and looked up at him and her green eyes were alight with mischief; she looked enchanting and his arms tightened about her.

'Don't tempt me,' she said, 'I thought we had buried the hatchet.'

'Yes,' he said, 'right between my shoulder blades.'

Laughter gurgled and she relaxed completely against him, and he smiled down at her, his eyes warm and glowing deeply.

'This is nice,' she said, luxuriously, secure and content in his arms, letting him lead where he willed.

'*You* are nice,' he said.

'Am I?' It was said dreamily, not provocatively.

'I thought I had proved that to you already.'

He felt her stiffen in his arms.

'We won't talk about that,' she said, very low.

'All right; but you can't stop me thinking about it.'

'Your thoughts are your own,' she said stiltedly.

'Would that they were.'

He was teasing her again but there was something else; an underlying wry resignation, an acceptance of something that could not but be accepted.

She looked up at him uncertainly, frowning a little, trying to catch hold of that fleeting something she had seen in his eyes but it had gone; now they only smiled down at her.

'I think you are flirting,' she said primly.

'And I think you like it.'

She grinned. 'I do.'

He laughed and the hand that held hers twined her fingers closely, his own warm and strong. He had beautiful hands; Jane always noticed hands. Bitten nails and nicotine stains she found distasteful. His were beautifully shaped, long fingered, square-tipped, the nails clean, no nicotine stains—not that he smoked a great deal. She thought of those hands and how they had caressed her and her whole body flamed at the memory because more than ever, she wanted him to do it again. But she had said they would not talk of that—but he had said he thought of it. As much as she did—which was constantly? She hoped so; fervently and devoutly she wished so.

Her sigh was soft, wistful, like the music, to which they drifted around the floor as though by some process of levitation. Jane loved dancing, especially with someone who knew what he was doing—and Luís de Capdevila was an expert. Dancing with him was a combination of pleasure and pain; it was marvellous to be held in his arms but it was not enough; it would never be enough. She wanted more; much more.

She gave herself up to the music, unable to resist the combination of being in Luís's arms, the sensuous beat of the rhythm and his dancing, which like him, was superb. It was pure instinct that made her relax, so that he drew her in closer, her face resting against his; cheek to cheek.

She closed her eyes and let herself drift, carried along on a wave of feeling, utterly abandoned and unconsciously and disturbingly provocative.

'Don't go to sleep on me,' Luís said lightly, but warningly. 'I have had to watch you being monopolized by every other man in the room all evening; now that I have got you to myself am I to be content with a Sleeping Beauty?'

'Not sleeping,' said Jane with a sigh, 'dreaming.'

'Of what?'

'If I tell you then it won't come true.'

'Do they ever?'

'One must hope so.'

'But have you not realized all your dreams? What more is there for you to prove.'

'Prove?' Jane frowned. 'I'm not trying to prove anything.'

'Really,' he said dryly. 'To quote you, my dear Jane —"You could have fooled me".'

'Perhaps I have been,' Jane said challengingly.

His eyes narrowed. 'I hope not,' he said softly.

'You'll never know, will you?' she asked flippantly. 'I'll be gone in another month and it won't matter any more.'

'To whom?' he asked his voice softer than ever.

She laughed then. 'Game, set and match,' she acknowledged. 'You and I always seem to have conversations that are rallies. But you've seen me play; you know I do it well.'

'Supremely well,' he admitted unsmilingly.

'So do you. But then, you must have had a lot of practice.'

He took her chin in his hand and made her look at him. 'Now that,' he said, 'is a double fault.'

She threw back her head and laughed, joyously, ringingly. People turned to stare, and more than one of them thought what a striking couple Luís de Capdevila and the English blonde made. One of them, in particular, thought it with hatred in her heart.

Luís' arms tightened. 'Jane, Jane . . .' he said reprovingly. 'What am I going to do with you?'

Love me! she cried silently. Love me! But she said lightly: 'I am not yours to do anything with. Besides, Queta might have something to say about that.'

'Queta?'

'Trained to obey,' Jane said innocently.

'You think so?'

She flinched at the coldness in his voice. Idiot, she raged at herself. Do you have to fly in the face of all his prejudices? Why can't you leave well alone ... But the devil inside her prodded her on relentlessly. 'Of course! If she was not she would not have waited around so long.'

'You would not, of course—wait, I mean.'

'Patience was never my strong point,' she admitted airily, thinking: For you—for ever.

'Nor is your tact,' he said curtly.

They danced in silence for a while, Luís' face dark and brooding. She had done it again! thought Jane. With her unfailing wrong sense of timing she had trampled all over a further section of forbidden territory labelled clearly 'KEEP OFF—THIS MEANS YOU' and had left unmistakable footprints all over it.

'I'm sorry,' she apologized gallantly. 'I seem to have done it again.'

He regarded her unsmilingly, almost grimly. 'Done what?'

'Strayed into forbidden territory. That's another fault of mine; I have absolutely no sense of direction.'

His mouth twitched and the darkness of his face was transformed by the brilliance of his smile. His laugh was genuine and unforced.

'Just so long as it brought you in mine,' he acknowledged smilingly.

Phew, thought Jane, you nearly wrecked that. Now,

keep your mouth shut and just dance.

When he finally took her back to her seat they were in perfect charity with each other and Jane was hoping he would ask to take her into supper when out of the blue, a familiar voice said laughingly: 'I knew it was you; nobody else looks like that or moves like that! Jane, love, how are you?'

She turned to look into the bright blue eyes and laughing countenance of a very tall, very blond man who could only be British.

'James! Oh, darling James!' she cried, hurling herself at him. 'Let me look at you!' She did, eyes sparkling, face radiant. 'Oh, James, you are a sight for sore eyes! But what are you doing here! I thought you would be in Scotland on the ancestral acres slaughtering grouse!'

'I will be—next week. Want to come along? My old man is for ever nagging me as to why I haven't got you under lock and key with the family ruby on your finger and the church booked!'

'Oh, James ...' Jane laughed up at him fondly, and hugged him again. 'I can't believe it—to have you turn up here, of all places—right out of the blue.'

'Just like the bluebird,' he said promptly.

He held her hands and looked at her. 'I must say, Jane love, you look absolutely marvellous. Something obviously agrees with you. You positively glow.'

'You always did pay the nicest compliments,' Jane said, kissing his cheek.

'The end I am after is twofold; you, and my father's dotage made happy by the acquisition of the future chatelaine of Airth Castle.'

'But you know I adore Airth,' protested Jane.

'Enough to take me with it?'

Jane laughed up at him lovingly. 'James, you know

you don't really want to settle down just yet ...'

'With you? Have a heart, love. Do I look crazy?'

Jane hugged him again and he put his arms round her and looked at Luís, who had stood by silently taking it all in.

'Sorry, Sir, if I am muscling in on your territory,' he said in English. 'But Jane is an old and a very bright flame. 'I'm James Creighton-Stuart.' He removed an arm from Jane and held out a hand, which Luís took.

'You are with your Embassy in Madrid aren't you?' he asked quizzically.

'Yes. I came here with the Montoyas. I'm staying with them this weekend.'

'I know the Montoyas.'

Jane came to with a start, remembering her manners. 'I am so sorry,' she said to Luís. 'The surprise of seeing James made me forget ... James, this is Señor Luís de Capdevila. I am tutoring his wards this summer.'

'What, still at it when you could be in Scotland with me?'

'Miss Elliot has made herself indispensable this summer,' Luís said dryly, eyes opaque and expressionless, 'but there is only another month to go. After that I am sure she will be delighted to shoot with you. She does it very well.'

'Doesn't she though! My father says Jane has the best eye he has ever seen.'

'I had already formed that opinion,' Luís said, still dryly.

'James is a very old friend,' Jane said quickly, 'we were at Oxford together, though he was a year or two ahead of me ...'

'Only chronologically,' said James grinning. 'She used to coach me too, Sir, to help me get through my exams.'

'Which you did, of course,' Luís said smoothly.

'Naturally. Jane has a way of making one understand and appreciate.'

'Something else I had noticed,' Luís said quietly. He turned to James. 'You must have a great deal to talk about. I wish you luck in your endeavours.' He bowed to Jane and went off leaving her looking after him, suddenly desolate. James watched her. He knew his Jane.

'Him?' he asked succinctly.

She met his eyes. 'Him.'

James sighed. 'Poor Father. He'll probably shoot *me*!' He put an arm about Jane's shoulders. 'Come along and tell old James all about it. I always did have one of the best shoulders in the business, and this is a nice clean handkerchief in my pocket ...'

Jorge and Alejandro were dismayed. At this time, to have an English *Milor* come along and monopolize Jane. It was too much. They said so.

'But he is an old friend,' said the Señora reprovingly. 'Jane said so when she introuced us. They were at university together.'

'There is more here than just an old friend,' Jorge said darkly. 'I know.'

'He is only here for the weekend,' chided his mother impatiently. 'He is going home to Scotland on Monday.'

'And wants to take Miss Jane with him; I heard him ask her,'

'And I just as clearly heard her refuse. Miss Jane told us she would remain with us for the entire summer. She is not the kind of person to break her word.'

'No, but he is the kind of person who would make her wish she could.'

This alarmed the Señora and she made a point of seeking out Jane to ask her.

'I do not wish to pry, you understand, but if you should particularly wish to go to Scotland with Lord James then we would not stop you...' she dimpled at Jane mischieviously. 'He is in love with you I think.'

'James!' Jane laughed. 'Oh, no. Not really. He pretends to be and we are very great friends—it is his father; he likes me and I know he would like us—James and I—to marry—but it is all a great joke between us; no more. I would not dream of leaving you before the end of September. I am too happy here...' And I could not leave Luís until I absolutely had to, she thought.

The Señora was reassured and content; not so Alejandro or Jorge. Both were instantly jealous; of the edge James had with Jane; of the mutual friends and old acquaintanceship; of memories re-lived, old times invoked. Jane would never allow either of them to act so familiarly; he called her 'love' and had the easy intimacy of someone not only privileged but special, and they eyed with resentment the way he danced with her—often and long—and worse still, went off with her to a dark corner of the terrace; something they had both tried to do without success.

'Why did he have to come along now?' complained Jorge bitterly to his Uncle Luís.

'He wants to marry her,' his uncle said shortly. 'I heard him say so.'

'But Mama says Miss Jane told her it is only a game they play...'

'On the surface, perhaps; but Lord James is playing a deceptively easy game... he will persist, and his father approves, even though he is not the eldest son. But Jane would still be Lady James Creighton-Stuart and the mistress of a beautiful castle in Scotland. The Montoyas tell me the Creighton-Stuarts own half the Highlands.'

'Money and titles mean nothing to Miss Jane,' said Jorge dismissively.

'I know that—but his father's approval might. English aristocrats choose their wives very carefully as a rule; that is why they have lasted so long: they seem not to change but they always move with the times—and the times have changed a great deal in England ...'

Jorge looked at his uncle strangely.

'You have obviously given the matter some serious thought,' he observed rather acidly.

'Naturally; we have all become very attached to Miss Jane this summer. It would be nice to think she made a good marriage and was happy.'

'You astonish me!' Jorge said. 'Since when have you cared what happened to former employees?'

His uncle flicked him with an ironic glance. 'Since Jane,' he said.

Jorge sighed. 'I know what you mean,' he said. 'She is remarkable, isn't she?'

'Too much for you,' Luís de Capdevila said shortly. 'I told you once before. You are wasting your time where she is concerned. Jane is not the kind to indulge in summer dalliance. That is not her way.'

'I did not mean to fall in love with her,' Jorge said miserably.

'She has that effect on one,' his uncle said expressionlessly.

They both looked out to where Jane and James stood on the terrace, James's arm around her waist in casual possession, she looking up at him with absorbed concentration as he talked to her, reaching up absently to brush back a lock of hair that would fall over his forehead.

'You need a haircut,' Jane said absently to James.

'We are not talking of me,' James said severely. 'I am taking the time and trouble to help you in your tangled love-life and my hair does not come into it. If you won't put me out of my misery I can at least try to put you out of yours.'

Jane giggled. 'You sound like a vet.'

James grinned at her. 'That's the worst of being brought up on a Scottish estate. You tend to equate the four-legged beasties with what really matters—which they do. If dear old Dad could not let the shoot every year to those rich Americans God knows what would become of us.'

'Already she treats him like a husband,' Jorge said tormentedly.

'Now then, what are you going to do about this Spaniard you have gone overboard for, young Jane? If you are having difficulty in bringing him up to scratch we shall have to apply the old beaters. What if I make a dead-set at that delicious-looking girl-friend of his? The one the Montoyas tell me has been stalking him for years...'

'Queta dos Santos,' Jane said miserably. 'But that would not work, James. In this country if you have a moral obligation you keep it come hell and highwater; you have given your word.'

'But has he love? Given it, I mean. From what I am told she is the one doing all the running.'

'But according to her brother it is an understood thing.'

'Good God! Do they still have them?'

In spite of her misery Jane had to laugh. 'Oh, James,' she said, putting her arms around his waist and leaning her head against his chest. 'You are such a comfort.'

'That is all you will allow me to be,' he said in mock-sorrow, 'but if that is what you want then I shall provide the best comfort in the business.' He dropped a kiss on the top of her head.

'You see!' Jorge turned tormentedly to his uncle. But his uncle had gone.

Some time later, Jane went into the bedroom that had been set aside for the ladies, to tidy her hair and splash her heated face with cold water. As she sat re-applying her lipstick Queta came up behind her.

'A word in your ear, Miss Jane,' she hissed, two spots of colour burning like warning flags in her cheeks. 'Your blatant pursuit of Luís de Capdevila is causing talk. I am aware you English girls have a great deal of freedom, but the Capdevilas have no need of such notoriety.'

Her eyes met Jane's in the mirror; they were burning too, stoked with her jealousy.

'I have not heard any talk,' Jane said coldly.

'Naturally not—since it is you everyone is talking about!'

'*I* do not know that they are,' Jane told her frigidly, 'nor do I see why you are making such a fuss over something that just simply isn't true ... In any case, I return to England in four weeks time and I doubt I shall see Señor Capdevila again.'

Her voice was steady though the thought was anguish.

'And just as well,' cried Queta. 'Here in Spain the men still do the pursuing; we have not yet reached your stage of so-called equality and exchanged roles.'

'You know nothing about it,' snapped Jane. 'You would not know what to do if equality was handed to you on a plate.' She knew she was being rude but she was cross and miserable and beginning to wish she had never taken on this job in the first place.

Queta drew in her breath with a hiss. 'You forget

yourself,' she said acidly.

'Never!' Jane met her eyes in the mirror. 'I know only too well who *I* am!'

Queta's hands turned into talons but she clenched them, and turning her back on Jane stalked away.

Jane leaned her head on trembling hands. She felt sick. She hated all this intrigue and flag-waving of emotions. It was not her way. She had *not* been pursuing Luís, nor he her ... well, all right; so he had kissed her, had flirted with her—but no more than that. It was Queta's sixth- even seventh-sense where he was concerned that was the cause of the trouble. She had sensed his interest in Jane: where Luís de Capdevila was concerned she would notice anything that posed even the slightest threat. The thought of the next four weeks filled Jane with apprehension. She prayed devoutly that she could get through them without some sort of major upset. Then she could go back home and try to forget Luís—if she could.

When she went back out to the party James came to her at once.

'I saw the girl friend follow you,' he said. 'If looks could kill, my love, you'd be cat's meat!'

'She came to do a little character assassination too,' Jane told him as lightly as she could, but he was not deceived. He knew his Jane.

'Custer's last stand?' he asked quizzically, blue eyes bright with the light of battle.

Jane's own great green eyes took up the torch.

'Let's really show 'em,' she vowed.

'Up the Scots!' exulted James, and hand in hand they made their way to the dance floor. There, they proceeded to show the applauding Spaniards what the English domination of 'pop' really meant; not for nothing had James and Jane been the best dancers of their day at university. No matter how driving the beat they were its masters, and as the other couples dwindled from the floor they were left to themselves in an effortless exhibition of grace and style that had an appreciative audience applauding and cheering for more.

Jane's natural sense of rhythm and grace had never showed to better advantage, and James—also a natural—matched her all the way. Even Jorge forgot his bitter-tasting jealousy in an instinctive response to such a masterly display of skill, which he admired in anyone, and joined in the enthusiastic response.

Finally, as the beat slowed to a deep, throbbing pulse, they came together in a last display of langorous elegance that had the Señora moist-eyed and lost in memories, and Jorge and Alejandro envying James so deeply that they were united, for the first time that summer, in a genuine, shared understanding.

The floating chiffon of Jane's multi-coloured skirt swirled round her in a slow-motion drift that formed sculptures in the air; the strobe lights rippled over them in an unearthly flow of liquid fire. Her hair became in turns pink, then blue, then silver; her face, upturned to James, smiling down at her, was dreaming and lovely, with almost unreal beauty.

'*Qué hermosúra*,' murmured someone.

Their feet hardly seemed to touch the ground; they floated, swayed, glided, drifted in a hushed, almost reverent atmosphere of evocative and provocative music and there was not a man in the room who did not wish he were in James' place or a woman who did not envy Jane.

Queta dos Santos was almost sick with hatred. Standing next to Luís de Capdevila she could feel his total concentration on Jane. It was he out there, not James Creighton-Stuart; he held her, he moved with her, his concentration was almost ferocious, as if willing her to move in his direction, and as if Jane responded to it, as she and James swirled over to where he stood Jane lifted her closed lids to look straight into his eyes. For a long electric moment they exchanged such a look, then James had turned her and they glided away to another part of the floor.

Queta could have screamed. Never, *never* had Luís looked at her remotely like that; so deeply, so palpably it was like his touch. She could have taken that look and wrapped herself in it. They gave themselves away with their eyes, said it all with their eyes; gazing, drowning, lost in what they alone could see.

With absolute clarity, Queta knew she had lost Luís de Capdevila—if she had ever had him. Her carefully planned future lay in ruins. He was committed to Jane Elliot, and she to him. That look had said it all; no need for words. Blinded by tears of desperate rage, Queta turned and made unseeingly for a quiet dark place in which to hide her agony, knowing even as she did so that Luís was not even aware of her going.

She had lost. And she hated.

Everyone slept very late next morning; it had been 4 a.m. before they got to bed. James had been invited for lunch and to accompany them that afternoon to the *tienta*.

Even though she had danced the night away Jane was awake early. The transcendental joy she felt would not let her sleep. Luís loved her! His eyes had told her so; so clearly, so unmistakably, in one marvellous, total exchange of mutual feeling and experience. It had shaken her to the central core of her being, but she knew; she felt it, took it to her and exulted in it. He had revealed it so openly, so nakedly, so much so that James, who was sensitive though his looks belied it, murmured triumphantly in her ear: 'Told you so.'

Through all the acclamation, the praise, the congratulations, she had only been able to stand by James and look across at Luís, on the fringe of the crowd, and his eyes had told her again. In another, no-holding back, composure-shattering look those onyx eyes had sent the message loud and clear. She had heard it inside her head: You are mine, it said, I love you. And into her mind had come something else, something she had forgotten in the heat of those moments in his arms. When he had been murmuring to her in Spanish he had addressed her by the intimate *tu*—thou—which was used only to children and those people closest and most intimate. She ought to have realized it then, but better late than never. Now she knew. No doubt at all. He did not come across to her. There were too many people and this was not the time. But she knew. They both did.

Lying in bed, Jane relived it all. It had been a very strange experience. A sort of extra-sensory perception, as though each had gone inside the other's mind. And James—dear James—had understood at once. He was a true friend.

She did not feel this morning, that over-riding desire to see Luís to reassure herself of his presence; wherever he was they were together. Whatever happened in the future they always would be. She would wait until he came to her to tell her in words what his eyes had made so plain.

He was not at breakfast; he had been called away early to the packing sheds by Manúel, but Jane was not worried. It only made his eventual appearance that much more satisfying and rewarding. She was happy to wait; happy and content. He loved her. That was all that mattered.

When James arrived before lunch he eyed her and said laughingly: 'Come down off that cloud. You are so far up there you'd break your neck if you fell!'

'I'm sorry James. It's just that—well, its all so marvellous! I never felt like this before! Requited love is so different from the unrequited sort.'

'You don't say,' marvelled James, struggling not to laugh. 'I can see I am going to have to keep an eye on you to stop you stepping into manholes and walking through plate-glass windows. You are just not safe to be let out alone, love.'

Luís had still not turned up by lunch-time but rang to say he would join them at the *ganadería* later that afternoon and to go on without him.

So after lunch, at about four o'clock, they all piled into the cars to drive the fifteen miles to where the *tienta* would be held, on the ranch of the Marqués de Puenteferísa.

The young calves about eight to ten months old, were in pens by the small white-walled ring, where the men, in leather chaps and broad-brimmed Cordobese hats, stood and chatted and made notes as to the capability of each youngster; their bravery, their skill, their speed. Queta, in a beautifully cut divided skirt and boots, with a short leather jacket and a hat like the men neither looked nor spoke to Jane, in denim jeans and a checked shirt and battle jacket. James wore the same and they made a striking pair; both tall, both blonde, both tanned.

Everyone perched on the wall around the ring to watch with interest as the youngsters were put through their paces. Both Jorge and Alejandro, in short jackets and chaps, effected a great knowledge of the procedures and talked knowledgeably of bulls; of their formation and size and bravery. Sherry was plentifully dispensed, and it was hot enough to cause Jane to dring three *copitas*; they, and Queta's barbed remarks, were her downfall.

After they had had their try with the calves, Jorge and Alejandro came back to rejoin the little group, whereupon Inés said scornfully: 'Jorge fancies himself as *El Cordobés*, but he would not even make a *novillero*, would he Miss Jane? Why, you could do better than him, I'll bet!'

'No thank you,' said Jane forcefully. 'I prefer to sit and watch.'

'You surprise me,' Queta sneered. 'I thought there was nothing you could not do, Miss Jane.'

'There isn't,' defended Inés instantly.

'Oh, come now,' protested the Señora comfortably. 'Testing calves is something which requires a knowledge and a skill Miss Jane does not possess.'

'I'll bet she could, Mama,' Inés said eagerly. 'Couldn't you, Miss Jane?'

'Of course she could not,' Queta said deliberately.

'Oh, I don't know,' Alejandro said thoughtfully. 'Miss Jane has a fantastic set of reflexes and perfect co-ordination. It is all a question of timing really ... perhaps with the smallest of the calves ... ? It really is something you should try, Miss Jane. Lots of people do. Especially tourists.'

'Be sensible Alejandro,' cautioned the Señora sharply. 'You know Luís would not allow it. These are not sheep —they are *vacas*; some of them big enough to cause real injury.'

'We would pick the smallest one, Mama,' Jorge said with bored patience. Really, his mother made such a fuss sometimes.

'That little brown one could do no harm—and Alex and I will show her clearly and carefully what to do.'

He got down from the wall. 'If the *Marqués* has no objection I do not see why you should,' he said reasonably and ignoring his mother's protests he was away across the ring in the direction of their host, who, having lived and breathed bulls all his life and taught his own children to do the same, could see no objection provided they showed the English Señorita exactly what to do and chose the smallest calf.

In a panic the Señora looked round the ring for James, but he had gone to look at the stud bull in the pens behind the testing ring and was nowhere to be seen. She wished Luís was here. He would soon put a stop to all this nonsense.

'Miss Jane, I don't think you should,' she said nervously.

'I don't think I should either,' Jane said cheerfully. 'So I won't.' The Señora relaxed. Jane was such a sensible child.

'So you *are* afraid of something,' jeered Queta viciously, her eyes glittering with hatred.

'Isn't everyone?' asked Jane pointedly.

'I have not seen you go into the ring against them, Queta,' the Señora told her tartly, wishing Queta would stop being so spiteful and more mindful of her manners.

'I do not pretend to be the equal of any man; I know my limitations,' Queta purred.

'So do I,' retorted Jane sweetly poisonous. 'That is what liberation is all about.'

'Either you are—completely—or you are not,' Queta dismissed contemptuously. 'You obviously are not, since you are afraid to demonstrate your liberty to the full.'

'I am!' cried Jane, stung.

'Prove it,' dared Queta cruelly.

'Please, Miss Jane,' cried the Señora desperately. 'And you too, Queta. Stop baiting Miss Jane. You are urging her to do something of which Luís would not approve and which could be dangerous.'

'But if she is the equal of any man then there can be no real danger . . . testing calves is a man's work, is it not . . . ?' Her smile was derisive. 'If she is not equal . . .'

'She is!' cried Jorge and Alejandro fiercely, both very partisan.

'Then let her prove it,' challenged Queta.

They turned to Jane expectantly. She hesitated. She did not see why she should have to do anything to prove herself to Queta dos Santos. She was not important enough. None of this was important enough. The only thing that mattered today was Luís—and if he would not approve, then that was all the more reason not to flout him—even today. But Jorge and Alejandro and the twins were looking at her with such obvious expectation and conviction in her abilities that she felt to refuse would let them down—but Luís was the one who counted.

'I don't think Señor Luís would approve,' she said doubtfully.

'A good excuse,' taunted Queta. 'You *are* afraid—you are not equal at all; you only pretend to be!'

That literally was the red rag. 'I am not afraid,' flared Jane.

'Then prove it,' pounced Queta.

'All right,' snapped Jane. 'I will.'

Before she knew where she was she was swept up in a gigantic snowball that swept her along with frightening momentum and almost before she knew it she was in the ring with Alejandro and Jorge instructing her how to hold the cape and cite the animal; how to stand, how to move, how to turn the charging youngster. They stood by her while she tried it several times and then, seeing her do it so well, they retired to perch on the wall and watch her, applauding and cheering her on.

'See,' said Inés contemptuously to Queta. 'I told you Miss Jane could do it.'

Queta stalked away stiff-backed.

Jane found it all great fun; it was exhilarating to have this beast—the size of a donkey but with horns—coming at you and to steer it round you by swirling the red and yellow cape in a graceful curve. After half a dozen passes she was convinced she was England's answer to Conchíta Cintrón, and James, brought back from the breeding pens by an anxious Señora, found to his horror that Jane was in the middle of the ring—alone—confronting what looked suspiciously to him like rather more than a calf!

Jane was too caught up in her own excited sense of prowess to notice that the animal had changed; that it was bigger, and pawed the ground and looked highly dangerous. But the others had and suddenly there were shouts of alarm and James began to run. So did Luís de Capdevila, coming across from where he had parked his car, to arrive at the ring and find to his appalled horror that Jane was citing a great, horned creature that charged her like an express train, and this time it did not turn. It went straight at her, and catching its horns in her jeans it hooked them and spun her like a top, the force of its rush ripping them open as it went by, hurling her to the ground, whereupon it turned on a *peseta* and came back at her. She had automatically, with her superb reflexes, curled herself up into a ball, arms shielding her head, but even so, before James—who had vaulted the wall—and a white faced Jorge and Alejandro ran forward, it had dug at Jane with its horns. Then they had drawn it away and there was pandemonium as everyone rushed forward shouting and yelling but a tall dark figure was already there, having vaulted the wall as James had done even as the bull had come back at her.

Jane was conscious but dazed. The right leg of her jeans was ripped right across but there seemed to be no blood. Quickly Luís felt her limbs and body for damage, his hands trembling but quite impersonal. She seemed uninjured but the doctor would have to say for sure.

After a few moments Jane opened her eyes and lay blinking up at them, then she saw it was Luís and smiled up at him drunkenly.

'Ooops!' she said thickly. 'I fumbled that one,' then she passed out.

She came to in the little infirmary the ranch maintained for such accidents, the doctor taking her pulse and the Señora hovering distractedly.

'Oh, Miss Jane,' she said with vast relief when she saw Jane open her eyes, before bursting into tears.

'Please. Señora ...' Jane tried to sit up but the room swam and her head hurt. So did her back. And her thigh. When she had hit the ground the breath had been knocked out of her. She winced.

'You are hurt,' moaned the Señora. '¡*Ay, Por Dios!* Luís will be so angry!'

'No—please. Don't distress yourself. I am not hurt; really I am not. Just shaken and bruised.'

'You are lucky to be alive! That was no calf, Miss Jane—that was a fully grown animal! Someone played a stupid trick on you and woe betide them when Luís finds out ... what he will say! ¡*Ay, Por Dios!*'

She wrung her hands and sobbed distractedly.

'It is not your fault. He will not be angry with you,' Jane said, feeling sick and dizzy.

'Oh, but he will—for allowing you to do such a dangerous thing. I know Luís!'

'But it was not your fault!' Jane said desperately. 'It was mine! I am responsible for my own actions. I will explain. He will understand.'

She was confident, though somewhat apprehensive. It had all been a joke, after all, even if it had got out of hand. She had thought that last calf looked rather large. Who on earth would want to play such a stupidly dangerous trick as that? Surely Luís knew her well enough by now to know she would not be so foolhardy as to go into the ring deliberately in front of a great horned creature like that! Dread paralysed her. Supposing that was exactly what he did think ... supposing Queta had told him exactly that—but he would not believe Queta, surely? The others would put him right. Besides, it was Jane he loved. Queta's mischief making, apparent all afternoon, was transparently clear now. Jane realized that she had been forced into that ring deliberately. Had Queta been responsible for the change of bull? Jane felt sickened. She really does hate me, she thought. I *must* get to Luís before she does. I have to make him see how it was before she can twist it round; make him see it all wrong ... she wants him herself and she'll do for me if she can. I have to get to Luís, to tell him ...

Her head spun and her thigh burned where the horn had creased it, but slowly, carefully, she sat up, putting her legs over the side of the bed, holding on tight with both hands because she felt dizzy and sick. She had to get up, to see Luís ...

'Please, Miss Jane! Do not move. You must wait for

the doctor to return. He has gone to reassure Luís that you are not badly injured.'

'But I must see Señor Luís—to explain. I am responsible for my own actions, Señora, but he must know why I did them.'

'You must not move,' begged the Señora. 'Please, lie back and rest.'

'It is not your fault,' Jane repeated muzzily. 'I will tell Señor Luís I did not heed you . . .'

'What else could be expected from someone who does not know the meaning of the word obey?' asked an icy-cold voice and Jane knew with sickening dread that it was too late. He stood in the room just inside the door, his face a white, rigid mask, his eyes like coals. He was in a towering temper and obviously very worked up. Jane bowed her head, unable to look at him, and sat awaiting his onslaught. Queta had got there first and he had believed her, obviously. So she said nothing, only sat shaking, unwilling to let him see her anguished tears.

'Alicia!' He jerked his head; the Señora scuttled from the room like a frightened rabbit with a last despairing look at Jane.

'You ought to be put over someone's knee and thrashed,' he said in a dispassionately controlled voice that flayed, 'like the inconsiderate child you are. You have taken your damned equality too far this time. Bulls are not men; they are not so easily controlled. They are dangerous and not for amateurs, even those who think they are equal to anything. I trust you think a sore head and some bruising are a small enough price to pay for having demonstrated—once again—how equal you are —to anything and anyone.'

Silent tears dripped down Jane's cheeks and onto her hands. She kept her head down, hands gripping the edge of the table.

'Well?' he demanded icily. 'Have you no word of apology to make? For the distress you have caused the Señora, the worry you have caused the *Marqués* and the disturbance you have created here this afternoon; persuading two besotted young men to let you try something they ought to have refused out of hand.'

It was not like that, protested Jane silently; it was not! But she said nothing. Her voice was buried under a crushing load of pain and grief, flattened and bereft of strength. How could he think this of her? How could he? He loved her! What had Queta told him that he should say these things to her?

'I do not hear your apology.' He bore down relentlessly.

'I'm sorry,' her voice was clogged with tears.

'I cannot hear you; yet you speak up loudly enough in defence of your equality.'

'Damn equality!' Her voice heaved aside the strangling pressure of her grief and broke through, raw with misery, thick with sobs. She raised a ravaged face to him and at the sight of it his own changed and the fear he had been containing by anger overwhelmed him, but she was too distraught to see.

'I'm sorry! I'm sorry! I'm sorry! Full to the brim and running over! Will that do?' she screamed at him, before burying her head in her hands and sobbing unrestrainedly. It was then, for the first time, because the sleeve of her jacket as she held on to the table had covered her thigh, that he saw the livid weal of the horn burn. His face convulsed with horror and pain and he took a step forward, putting out a hand but just then the doctor bustled in.

'Ah, Señor de Capdevila—I was looking for you.

Nothing serious—some bruising and she was winded; worst of all is the horn burn. It is a nasty one but I will treat it and give her something for the pain. She is a brave girl—a day's rest and she will be as good as new...'

He went over to Jane and Luís dropped his hand and stood looking at Jane, his face white and agonized. She had her own hands over her face and shoulders were heaving.

'Now then, Señorita,' the doctor said kindly, doing what Luís longed to do, putting his arm around her. 'You have had a nasty shock,' he said soothingly, 'I will give you something to calm you down...'

Luís closed his eyes as if he could not bear to look then he turned on his heel and went out, striding past James, hovering outside anxiously without even seeing him.

SIX

Jane did not return to Cañas until later that evening. She had sobbed herself into a highly emotional and exhausted state and the doctor had given her a sedative. James had stayed behind to wait for her, and it was he who drove her back; very subdued, very pale, deeply unhappy.

'I will come to Scotland with you James, if the invitation still stands,' she said wearily.

'You know it does love; it is an open one,' James said warmly. 'But are you sure running away is the right thing to do?'

'I can't stay here,' Jane answered, low voiced. 'I can't! He holds me in complete contempt.'

'Ah, well. I intend to say a few words to him about that,' said James darkly. 'We all know who is responsible for his attitude and who it is has fed him slow poison.'

'No, please,' Jane said quickly. 'If he doesn't know me well enough by now not to believe all sorts of lies and twisted half-truths then there is no point.'

'Oh, but there is, love! You didn't see him when he carried you in. He was out of his mind with fear for you! I saw him! I think he thought that ruddy great beast had done for you and he was in a dreadful state. I honestly don't think he knew what he was doing or saying.'

'Oh, he knew all right,' Jane said bitterly.

'I still think he needs straightening out—and I shall do my best to do so.'

'It would not do any good; it never really was any good from the start. Just—some sort of summer magic. Not enough for a lifetime. We could never have a life together. It would never stand the strain.'

She stared blindly out of the car window, not seeing anything but her own misery. All the high, bright hopes of the night before—of that morning—were dead; blighted before the icy blast of Luís de Capdevila's anger, and the rot of her own stupidity. What really hurt was that Luís should believe Queta. Could he not tell the real from the false? She would have sworn he could. But that was before this afternoon. His words had stripped away her pride in layers. She sighed heavily.

James took his hand from the wheel and covered hers.

'What can I say, love? I wish I knew. But you know how I feel, don't you?'

'Dear James,' Jane's voice was ragged. 'What would I have done without you? Thank God you were here.'

They rode the rest of the way in silence.

The Señora wept when Jane told her of her decision. One look at Jane's white-faced desolation was enough to tell all. That look had been on another face she had looked at earlier that evening.

'I have destroyed it,' Luís had told her in black despair, not three hours earlier, after an abject group consisting of Jorge, Alejandro and the twins, had gone to him and told him what really happened. 'The one thing in my life I have wanted more than anything I have ever known. She sat there and never said a word in her own defence while I tore her in pieces—with a horn burn an inch wide that must have hurt like hell! What in God's name have

I done? I've hurt her beyond repair, Alícia; out of my own rage and fear and pride. I've killed any love she had for me—and she did love me; it was there—in her eyes, last night. I was going to ask her to marry me today. She was the delight of my life; all that spirit and courage and gaiety and absolute trustworthiness; why in God's name did I accept what Queta said as truth. If I had only thought for one moment...'

'You were in no fit state to think,' the Señora said soothingly, her own tears overflowing.

'But I should have known,' he said savagely. 'I know we fought at first; but that was what I loved about her; she had the courage of her own convictions and it did not take me long to find out that she has not a vicious thought in her head. What she does she does naturally, instinctively —and doesn't she do it well!' Pride briefly lit the sombre voice. 'I should have known that Jane never goes beyond her own capabilities; it is because they are so considerable that I leapt like a fool to the wrong conclusion...'

'You were pushed there—by Queta,' the Señora said firmly. 'She taunted Jane in a very vicious way—she *wanted* Jane to be hurt. ¡Ay, Por Dios! that a friend of mine—a former friend of mine—should do such a thing!' The Señora threw up her hands in horror.

'That does not alter the fact that I believed her when a few seconds consideration of the real facts would have shown me otherwise.'

'You were so worried and anxious you were not thinking straight,' said the Señora, trying to comfort.

'Worried! I was terrified! I thought she might have had internal injuries... that she might die. I could not see beyond the fact that she was hurt—and then, when I knew she was not—instead of thanking God on my knees fasting I lost my temper and gave her a verbal beating!

She must hate my guts.'

'I do not think so,' said the Señora gently.

'She trusted me,' he said. 'When Jane trusts there are no half-measures. I've let her down—badly. She'll never trust me again. I've destroyed it.'

He sighed. 'I'll leave Cañas this evening and not return during the rest of the summer. It will be for the best. Jorge and the children will not want to lose her—nor will you. It is enough that I have lost her.'

'But I am sure you have not!' cried the Señora despairingly. 'Jane loves you! Why should you think she would not be able to forgive you?'

'It is not *her* forgiveness I doubt; it is that I cannot forgive myself.'

He looked at his sister-in-law. 'You will let me know how she—does.'

'I will do anything that will bring you together again.'

'Then do it, Alícia,' his face, voice, were urgent, desperate. 'Do it!'

Now, the Señora looked at the duplicate of that misery and despair and burst afresh into bitter tears.

'Oh, Miss Jane! What have you done to each other?'

Jane put her arms around the small, unhappy figure.

'Please,' she begged. 'I cannot bear to see you so upset. We are adults, Señor Luís and I; we will get over it!'

'But there is no need! You love each other, I know, I know this; I have seen it. Why then cannot you overcome this? It is that Luís feels he has let you down badly and you no longer can trust or depend upon him—and this is important to such a man as he. I told you he was a hard man; this applies to himself as well as others: he cannot forgive himself for hurting you so badly. But he is so unhappy, Miss Jane. I have never seen him like this before.'

She sobbed broken-heartedly, an emotional lady of great sensibility who hated to see others unhappy.

'If you would only talk to each other!' she wept.

'About what? My foolhardiness or his gullibility?'

'But Queta told him such terrible lies about you; that the whole thing was your idea; that you laughed at me when I told you he would not approve; that you said you did not care what he thought—that he did not matter. She filled him with such doubts—made him think your beliefs about equality mattered more to you than he did. She was eaten up with jealousy. She has always hoped to marry Luís, you see. He has known her all his life; before he met you it was assumed they would eventually marry . . . he did not love her but she was suitable.'

'Whereas he loves me but I am not suitable.' Jane smiled mirthlessly.

'No, no!' protested the Señora. 'I cannot think of anyone more suited to Luís! In any case that would not matter to him if he loved someone enough—and he does love you, Miss Jane. I know this.'

'It would never work,' Jane said dispiritedly. 'We come from opposite poles; we live our lives on different planes and when you wear the rose-coloured glasses of love you are apt to lose your way between them and fall and hurt yourself.'

'But he was so unhappy and distressed when he found out the truth; when he realized he had misjudged you so badly. Can you not forgive him?'

'Easily, willingly, gladly.' Jane tried to swallow the hard lump that blocked her throat. 'What we cannot forgive, dear, kind Señora, is ourselves.'

Alejandro came to see her, very white, very subdued, almost abject. Luís had made his opinions plain in a few short words before he left.

'I am leaving this evening but I could not go before telling you how bad I feel about what has happened. That my own sister ... I had no idea she hated you so much. She knew of the danger—but she still did it! I would never have believed ...'

'It is all over and done with,' Jane told him tiredly. 'I did not have to go into that ring—but I did. Therefore I must take the consequences.'

Jorge, just as white, just as shaken, for he too, had had a session with Luís, added his pleas to Alejandro, begging Jane not to go, pleading with her almost tearfully. But to no avail.

It was the children who made it hardest. They came into her room and put their arms round her, crying silently.

'Don't go away, please, Miss Jane,' whispered Inés. 'We love you, Miss Jane. Please stay with us.'

'We will be good,' promised Luisíto, big brown eyes welling.

'You were always good,' whispered Jane, her own eyes filling up and spilling over.

'Then you will stay?'

'I can't.'

'Why not?'

'I have made your Uncle Luís very angry.'

'But we do sometimes and we do not have to go away.'

'I am not his niece or his nephew.'

'But Uncle Luís likes you, so why should he send you away?'

'He is not sending me, but I think it best that I go.'

'But you always told us his bark was worse than his bite,' Inés said, practical as always.

'I had not felt his bite then,' Jane said ruefully.

Inés was horrified. 'He bit you?'

'Not with his teeth; only with sharp words.'

'But I am sure he did not mean them,' Inés assured her tearfully.

'He was cross because of what happened at the *tienta*,' Luisíto said shamefacedly. 'He said we should not have done it. We told him we said you should, you see. But that was with the little bull—not the great big *toro*; that was Queta. She told the *mono* it was all a joke.'

'Some joke,' Jane said, trying hard to smile.

'Uncle Luís was very angry with her. She went after she spoke with him. She was crying.'

'Everyone is going away,' Inés said desolately. 'Uncle Luís has gone to La Menja—our other *finca* in the mountains. If he was here he would not let you go.'

'I do not think he would object,' Jane said sadly.

'But he knows we love you so why would he wish you to go,' Inés sobbed.

'It is for the best,' Jane said unsteadily.

'But it is not; not for us,' Inés argued practically through her tears.

'Are you and *Tío* Luís not friends any more?' Luisíto asked, troubled.

'No,' said Jane, her voice breaking under the strain, 'I am afraid we are not.'

They threw their arms around her and wept bitterly.

It was very hard for Jane, but harder still it would be to face the icy-eyed, hard-voiced stranger she had seen that afternoon, even if he now realized his mistake, even as she had realized hers. But she could not compound the error by driving him from his own house. She must be the one to leave.

So, with desolation in her heart she heaved out her cases and began to pack. There was nothing else to do. She had helped destroy everything else. All the radiant happiness of the night before, the glorious awakening only that morning—was it only hours ago—now it was all dead; ashes and dust in the mouth. Dry-eyed and dead-hearted she went methodically about the business of packing up the debris of that wonderful summer; the best in her life. The sea shells from the Cape; the bottle of champagne she had won at the *Tiro*; the souvenirs of the *Fiesta*; the seahorse—for Luisíto had insisted she take it when he was unable to keep it alive any longer. It was like a tiny, perfect jewel in her hand; turned to petrified stone like her heart. All these she packed away, with memories she could not yet bear to face; the white dress she had worn the night Luís had kissed her—better not think about that. The pretty rose-coloured one she remembered from the night she had realized she loved him; the swirling blues and greens of the night before when they had looked at each other and told each other—without words—that they loved. Or so she had thought. Only his love had not been strong enough to overcome his prejudices or to hold out against what he should have known—without a second thought—were lies ... could one truly love what one disapproved of? Hardly. But she could not think about it now. It was too painful. Best only to get away. To leave with James in the morning and go with him to Scotland, to a different world; back to her own kind, who knew her and understood and did not disapprove.

He would not like her running away, of course; breaking her contract. He would never do that. But she also knew he would not hold her to something no longer supportable. What had happened could not be overlooked; both felt guilty and that guilt would chafe and irritate until it could be covered over thickly and smoothly as the oyster covered its irritant grain of sand. This would not result in a pearl but it would not hurt any more.

When her packing was done it was just 8.30. Dinner was never before 9.30. That gave her an hour to say goodbye to the places she had come to love. It was dusk; the lovely half-light of the valley. She went downstairs and out on to the terrace. The valley was quiet, a haze hanging over it from the fires of the houses cooking dinner; the smell of ripening fruit hung heavy. Harvesting would begin soon, but she would not see that, nor taste the fresh figs from the tree at the back of the house. A dog barked some where, far off, and she could hear the soft cooing of the wood-pigeons. Hands deep in her pockets she walked down past the stables, where she went in to kiss goodbye to her sandy colt; she went, too, to the big chestnut Luís rode, stroked his glossy, arched neck.

'I *could* have ridden you,' she told him, 'but I never will now.'

Then she walked down to the tennis courts, remembering the hard, fast games of tennis with Jorge and Alejandro, the children cheering them on, and the patting of the ball back and forth with the children themselves. And the games of croquet. She went on to the swimming pool, stood there for a while, looking at it, calm and still, a few dead leaves floating on its surface. As she stood she was suddenly filled with an intense longing to see for the last time her favourite spot at Cañas—the marble swimming pool. She looked at her watch. 8.45. There was still time—especially if she took a jeep. She walked quickly back to the garages. A jeep stood ready and waiting, as always. In a moment she was in it and driving out of the yard.

Switching on the lights of the pool she walked slowly round it.

This was her favourite place in the valley. She loved

its peace, its quiet coolness, a combination of the marble statuary and the trellised vines that had grown right across it, forming a green canopy so that you bathed in shady coolness; a green grotto even at the peak of the day.

Even now, the marble benches outside were faintly warm from the day's sun. She sat for a while, mulling over the last three months, reliving the happiness, the good times, the pleasure; remembering—for memories were all she would ever have now—the feel of Luís; his mouth, his hands, his body; picturing the brilliant eyes, the dazzling smile; hearing the dark voice, the way it could be soft as silk one moment; iron hard the next.

She sat for a long time, weeping soundlessly, wishing desperately things could have been otherwise, then she wiped her eyes and looked at her watch. Almost 9.30. Time for dinner. Her last dinner at Cañas. Sighing, she stood up and turned to go back to the jeep when something thick and heavy was flung over her head, and big hands and an enormous body swept her off her feet. Her yell was cut off by the muffling cloth. She fought and kicked and jabbed with her elbows, but whatever held her captive had enormous strength and it was futile. She fought for air; the thick, heavy cloth was suffocating. Kicking out she hit shins, then she was lifted right off her feet, slung over a shoulder like a sack of potatoes and her breath cut off; a red mist opened up in front of her and she fell right into it, slumping against her captor, unconscious.

Luís de Capdevila drove the seventy miles from La Menja in a white heat of fear and desperation. The Señora's frantic telephone call telling him Jane was missing had come just after midnight, rousing him from the black pit of despair he had apathetically fallen into. He drove as fast as he could without taking foolish risks; it would not to do to kill himself now. But why, in God's name, had not Alícia telephoned him at once, instead of allowing wasted hours to elapse in a futile search of house and grounds, before ringing James to find out if Jane had gone to him because one of the jeeps was missing. But she had not; James had arranged to collect her next morning to drive her to Seville where they would catch the plane for London together. This last piece of painful news had decided Luís. Once Jane was found he would not let her go again, no matter what; if he had to tie her down and face those green eyes spitting fire and hear her saying out loud what her eyes had said that afternoon in the Calle de Velásquez; that he was an arrogant, overbearing, stiff-necked, male-chauvinist-pig of a Spaniard crammed full of prejudices and foregone—if outdated—conclusions—then he would do so; just so long as he had another chance to tell her he loved her and wanted her and to hell with pride, forgiveness, equality, anybody's liberation or anything else. Jane was all that mattered. Whatever she wanted to do, to be, to think, to say—just so long as it was with him.

But when he arrived at Cañas, to find James already there, Jane was still missing. The valley had been roused, the jeep found by the marble pool, plus a pocket-handkerchief under one of the marble benches; not some tiny scrap of useless lace; that was not Jane. This was a sensibly sized square of Irish linen with a J in one corner; the right size for blowing noses and wiping eyes. Luís pocketed that, feeling its dampness. She had been crying.

Sick with fear and self-loathing Luís raged at himself. Fool, fool! Is this what you have driven her to? Jane, of all people! With all her courage and spirit. My lovely Amazon, he thought wracked with guilt. What have I done to you?

Questions darted through his mind. The jeep was unmarked, so no accident. She must have gone somewhere on foot. What if she had fallen somewhere in the dark; in a ditch, a gully, down the mountain? No—Jane was fleet of foot and not the kind to wander off blindly. Taken, then? She had told him something or someone watched her. Were they responsible? Had someone been eyeing her greedily all summer, watching and waiting their chance? He would kill them if they had touched her. If any harm came to Jane ... he resolutely put from his mind the hideous thought of her at the mercy of some brute with rape on his mind ...

James noticed the expression on his face and, perceptive as he was, understood his thoughts.

'Look, sir. One thing I know for sure; if anyone has taken Jane they have a fight on their hands. She'll give them hell. She's not the type to faint or have a fit of the vapours; she is a strong, healthy, capable girl. If there is any way—any way at all—she can let us know where she is, she will do so. She once got lost when she was out on the moors with us; a mist came up in the way they have up there and suddenly you could not see a hand in front of you. Instead of wandering off blindly and maybe falling down a crag into a burn she just sat tight and waited, alternatively shouting and whistling—Jane's a crack whistler; hear it for miles—which is what we did do. So we found her. And we will this time, sir. You'll see.'

Luís smiled at him but it was merely a movement of the mouth.

'You are a remarkable boy, James. No wonder Jane is so fond of you.'

'Not fond enough, sir. It's you she wants.' James

grinned. 'My old man will be livid; Jane had him hooked and gaffed first time they met. I could never persuade her, though. Whereas you; I never saw Jane like this before...'

He paused fractionally then plunged in. 'This business of the bull...'

'My fault,' said Luís, 'first to last. I acted like a fool; I *was* a fool. I can only plead temporary insanity whilst under the influence of fear that Jane had been badly injured.'

'She thinks you have the lowest possible opinion of her; that's what she can't get past; she can't bear to feel she has let you down. Jane doesn't do that sort of thing.'

'So I have learned—the hard way,' Luís said quietly.

James felt reassured. It was obvious Luís cared deeply for Jane; why else would he look so hag-ridden, obviously strung up like an overwound tennis racquet.

The Señora had been expecting the lash of her brother-in-law's tongue; this suffering, white-faced automaton was no one she knew. The children huddled together, holding hands. Jorge and Alejandro—who had not left when Jane was found to be missing—were silent and obedient.

Both pools were dragged: nothing. They searched all night with dogs and lights; shouting and calling her name in case she was lying somewhere, or hurt or injured. By first light they all came trickling back to the house, which had been established as H.Q. No one had anything to report. Jane had vanished.

When Jane recovered consciousness she was lying on hard ground in total darkness. She had no idea where she was. Trying to sit up she heard the clink of metal as something pulled at her wrist and ankle. Feeling down she realized with sick horror that she was chained. For a moment panic swept over her and she screamed wildly, but her screams were oddly muffled in a thick, walled silence. She sat breathing deeply, trying to calm herself. Muffled screams equals small place, she reasoned. No light therefore no sort of window. Not a house then, nor a hut. What then? She was still fully dressed, her watch on her wrist. It had an illuminated dial. She could lift her hand as far as her waist and managed to look at it. 3.30. A.m. or p.m.? She decided it was a.m. If it was daylight there would be some indication of daylight somewhere; there had to be a door, surely. Was it underground? Better not think of that. The thought of being buried somewhere terrified her. Her mouth was dry. She was thirsty. She had not eaten since lunch—when—yesterday? Where was she—and why? Who had brought her here—and what for? Think, Jane, and don't panic, she told herself. They will be looking for you. They know you would not go off without saying goodbye. Anyway, your luggage is still at the house. And the jeep—perhaps that is still at the pool. If they find it they will know you must be somewhere near. If I am near, she thought uneasily. And always supposing whoever brought me here has not taken it. Was this a kidnapping? Not Queta again? Hardly. This was not her style; she was poison rather than a blunt instrument. But what if it was some kind of revenge? Ridiculous. Queta was not that stupid. She had already scuttled herself where Luís de Capdevila was concerned—ah, yes, but didn't that mean she had nothing to lose? Watch that imagination, Jane, she told herself. But what if she had been brought here to be left—not ever to be found? . . . she shut her mind to that before panic unhinged her.

She sat for a long time, thinking and wondering,

re-arranging the pieces in as many patterns as she could but none of them made sense. When she tried to move around and found the chains would not let her move more than feet rather than yards, in a sort of circle away from what she was discovered was a rock into which they were driven; she went wild for a few moments, heaving and pulling on the chains like a wild animal. Then she lay huddled for a while before getting on her knees to make a flat-handed floor-patting search of her immediate vicinity. She encountered only loose twigs and brush; and there was a smell of pines and eucalyptus. So she was still on the mountain. At Cañas? But where, in Cañas? It was 4,000 acres; Luís had told her. That was a lot of ground. But they would be searching. She was sure of that. Perhaps if she shouted. She did so, until she was hoarse and exhausted. Finally, she drifted into an uneasy doze.

She was awakened by a noise of bushes being rustled, and as she looked towards its source she saw daylight slowly lighten what was a cave entrance, about thirty feet away. Light increased as more bushes and finally a big rock were pulled away. And then, finally, a figure, stooped low, came through the entrance towards her. Rigid with terror she feigned sleep; looking through a fringe of lashes at whatever or whoever it was. It was a huge man; she saw him take a dumpy candle from his pocket and set it on a ledge; then he produced matches and lit it. The light revealed an enormous mountain of a man with the slack jaw, lolling tongue and empty eyes of a cretin. Fear drained her of strength and she lay limply. He came over to her and bent down; he smelled of garlic and sweat and stale clothes. He felt the chains—checking to see they were secure. Then he felt in his pockets and produced a cloth-wrapped bundle which he placed on the ground next to her. Beside it he placed a leather *bota*.

Next he bent over Jane. She did not move. Finally he did a very strange thing; squatting down he began to stroke her hair, which was spread about her like a skirt. He did it with the gentlest touch imaginable, and as he did so he crooned to himself. He lifted it and held it to his cheek and let it run through his fingers; he stroked it and kissed it and smelled it and lifted it and let it fall. He did this for about five minutes whilst Jane lay rigid. Then, still crooning to himself, he got up. He blew out the candle, but left it where it was. Then he went back down the cave and out into the light. She heard the thud of the rock, then the scrape of bushes again as the darkness became absolute once more.

She lay still for a long time, in case he came back, then sat up stiffly. It was not cold in the cave but it was clammy and the ground was hard. Looking at her watch she saw it was 7 a.m. Lifting the bundle she unwrapped it; it contained a thick wedge of what she recognized as the bread baked in the village, and a hunk of *chorizo*. The *bota* contained *vino tinto*; she fell on both with alacrity. She could think better on a full stomach.

Back at the house Luís was organizing a wider, much more detailed search. He had not slept. Every man had been drafted, estate workers as well as neighbours. All outbuildings had been searched; the stables, the garages, the storehouses, the packing sheds. Now they would have to concentrate on the estate itself; the woods and the mountains. They had already been right through the valley floor.

He had the big estate map on his desk; thousands of hectares of land he was marking into sections—each to be toothcombed. He was now beginning to be really afraid. He had to face the fact that Cañas was full of nooks and crannies where an injured girl could lie unconscious and unseen long enough to die. There were also the many mountain caves. All would have to be searched. And it all took time—too much time. She had already been gone twelve hours. Where was she? Where?

Jorge came in to find him studying the map as if to find answers and tried to reassure him. He had never seen his uncle look so white and strained. He looked, thought Jorge, as if he was suffering the tortures of a particular fiendish part of hell.

'Jane has tremendous courage,' he said stoutly. 'That was why she went in to the calves; only then it was nothing but courage for she truly did not know what she was doing—and I accept all the blame for that,' he proclaimed nobly. 'One thing I know; wherever Jane is—whatever has happened to her—she will not be afraid.'

'You think so,' said his uncle expressionlessly. He sat with his hands clasped loosely on top of the map. 'If we do not find her today I am calling in the police.'

They did not find her. By that night, when she had been gone twenty-four hours, Luís called the police. He looked driven. The Señora worried about him. She knew he was blaming himself. He had neither rested nor slept since the night of the engagement party; more than thirty-six hours.

'You must try to get some rest,' she pleaded. 'You cannot go on for ever.'

'I am not tired. I cannot sleep anyway.'

All he saw when he closed his eyes was Jane; Jane on the sandy colt casting covetous eyes at his chestnut stallion—which he had not doubted for a moment she could ride—and damned well—like everything else she did. He had wanted to provoke her—hadn't he? Testing out that freedom-loving, dare-accepting spirit of hers. Or Jane in the breakers at Cabo de los Angeles—like some sleekly beautiful sea-creature; Jane the first time he had seen her, straight backed and proud before turning on him in cat-eyed spitting fury, defending her beliefs; Jane romping with the children, lighthearted and gay and totally absorbed with them and in them—absolutely trustworthy and dependable; he had never had a single qualm where they were concerned; had seen how they adored Jane and obeyed her without question; Jane fending off Jorge in the nicest yet firmest way; Jane with her glorious hair braided with multi-coloured flowers—never in his life had he seen anything so beautiful; Jane in his arms in that clinging white dress—the feel of her, the scent of her, the flower-like unfolding of her mouth under his, terrifyingly passionate yet wholly innocent, offering herself in such a way as to make it so difficult to step back: and the final image—the desolate, tear-sodden face, the pain in those drowned eyes, and that livid weal on the golden skin of her thigh.

'All the courage in the world,' Jorge had said, and it was true; if Jane committed herself to you there was nothing she would not dare.

He had to find her; he *had* to. Not to do so was something he could not face. She had to be somewhere on the estate. She had been at the pool; the jeep had been left there—and the handkerchief. He took it from his pocket. Dry now, crumpled. It had been wet with her tears when found. He clenched his hand round it. His lovely Amazon. How that word fitted her. He would find her. He *would*.

Jane spent that day alternately dozing and shouting. It was useless to pull against the chains. They were too firmly fixed; she could move only in a limited circle. By the time her captor came back that night she was ready to plead; but he took no notice. He smiled at her and brought more food and wine and made signs for her to eat and it was then she realized he was a deaf mute; he could neither hear nor speak. That realization plunged her deep into despair with a block of cement tied to her ankles. She sat in dumb apathy as he stroked her hair and played with it. Obviously that was what fascinated him; why he had brought her here. He made wordless sounds of pleasure as he played with it, as though it were some rare and exotic animal. He had her chained up like some pet because he was attracted by the colour of her hair!

She spent Monday night in a state of almost numb desperation.

When Tuesday dawned she was lying facing the cave entrance and watched the light, never very strong, but stronger surely, today, because he had not rolled the rock back so closely, reveal that the cave was in reality a short tunnel opening out into a small rock chamber. A heap of brushwood lay in one corner, with some rags. An old wicker basket lay nearby and—she sat up—was it—dear God let it be—a flattened and dirty once-pretty box; the kind that carried matches. He always lit the candle when he came and blew it out when he left, but he took the matches with him. Lying flat she stretched out her free arm but her fingers fell about six inches short. She could reach the brushwood, though, and dragged out a longish piece with which she managed to scrape the box towards her. It contained four matches; flattened and trodden on but unused! Now she could have some light. Then—no—she thought—better wait. He might notice she had been burning the candle. He was a cretin but they could be cunning. Better play dead; hide the matches. Where? On her? He never touched her apart from her hair. She took them from the box so that they did not rattle, placing the matches in one pocket of her dress, the box in the other. Then she sat and thought. She had taken in the loose brush; holly-leaves, pine cones, bits of twig; all quite dry. It should burn easily and smoke a lot, especially if she sprinkled on a handful or two of pine needles. If the smoke could drift out of the cave—and please God let there be enough draught coming through the not-quite blocked entrance—it would rise on the warm air and hang there—the way it did in the valley; there was rarely enough wind to blow it away. But she would have to wait until he had been for his morning visit; endure his playing with her hair . . .

As she sat there making plans and feeling for the first time since her capture that at last she had some hope of getting out of this, she heard a deep, throbbing roar overhead. A plane—a helicopter! They were looking for her! Luís would have organized everything; she had every confidence in him. Whatever else had happened he would not rest until she was found; she knew that. And once she got that fire going . . . she looked at her watch. Just gone 6 a.m. *He* came at 7 a.m. She had an hour. Now—no time to lose—get that fire lit and smoking before that plane went away . . .

Luís met the police when they came with their tracker dogs, walkie-talkies and a helicopter, and explained the position and what he had done so far. He was bending over the map with the senior officer when the helicopter reported back at about 6.15 that it had spotted smoke in the rocky mountain-terraces at the back of the woods by the abandoned saw-mill. Luís had no men in that area.

The officer saw his face blaze with hope. 'That will be her,' he said, confidently.

'How can you be sure?' the officer was doubtful.

'She is a very resourceful girl . . .' Luís said in a voice that brooked no argument. 'I'll ride over—it's quicker. You follow on with the men by jeep. I'll meet you there.'

He ran for Castaña; the saw-mill was right at the back of the estate and fifteen minutes hard riding. It was long since abandoned and deserted for the river had dried up, but he knew it well. The mountain that rose behind it was honeycombed with caves he had played in as a boy. What better place to hide a captive?

As he neared the mill he could smell the smoke, hanging on the still air. All looked quiet; he could see and hear no one. He tied Castaña to the broken wooden fence and went forward towards the smoke; it was acrid, stinging, and coming from the mountain. He had taken down —instinctively—a hunting rifle from the rack in the gun-room, and now held it ready as he went forward quietly. If any harm had come to Jane he would shoot whoever was responsible. He could feel white-hot rage building inside him.

It was quiet in the trees; no noise but for the rustle of animals and birds.

Luís moved soundlessly. He had hunted these woods all his life and knew them well. At the back of the mill the rocky terraces rose steeply, honeycombed with caves and passages; a veritable maze of them. Jane must be in one of them. Who else would light a fire—a dead giveaway on this still air. He could smell it more strongly now, burning leaves and brush, see the grey-white smoke rising above the trees. He made his way towards it and as he came out of the woods he saw him; a giant of a man frantically hurling brush in all directions from what seemed to be a cave entrance. Luís recognized him.

'Oso . . .' he breathed, and suddenly all was clear. From

the cover of the trees he watched the huge bear of a man—his name, Oso, meant bear—roll away the heavy boulder which blocked the entrance, allowing smoke to billow rather than drift out, then disappear inside. Luís followed him, rifle at the ready. The smoke was thick; stinging the eyes. He could hear movement and coughing from inside the cave—two people. Then he heard the voice he loved.

'Stop it you big oaf—ouch! You idiot—you are tearing my hair out by the roots! Will you let go!' Feet stamped and metal clinked.

Luís grinned exultantly. She was all right; obviously in a temper and full of spirit. Instantly he was in the tunnel and along it to the rock chamber. And there they were; the giant had Jane by the hair and was attempting to stamp out the smouldering fire whilst Jane struggled to prevent him, not able to do much because she was chained. Luís felt anger blast him like a bolt of lightning. He shot the bolt of the rifle.

Jane turned at the sound and saw him; her face blazed and she shouted his name in a voice that evaporated all his anger and fear.

'Luís . . . !'

Oso turned, let go of Jane and came towards Luís, bear-like arms outstretched, and Luís shot him in the leg. Even before Oso hit the ground Luís had Jane in his arms, holding her tight, face filthy and stained with tears caused by the acrid smoke which was also making his own eyes stream, both of them trembling with reaction and relief and the sheer joy of each other again.

'Oh, my love,' he said, 'what has he done to you? Are you all right?' He looked at her anxiously but she smiled at him radiantly yet reassuringly, a sparkle of mischief in her eyes. She was still full of spirit.

'I know you believe in obedience, Luís,' she chuckled, in a hoarse, wobbly little voice quite unlike her usual clear contralto, 'but isn't this taking things a little too far . . . ?'

His laugh was exultant as he gathered her to him again.

'My beautiful, resourceful Amazon,' he said in a choked voice. 'I knew it was you when I heard they had sighted smoke. How did you do it—rub two sticks together?'

His voice was teasing yet full of pride and love.

'I could have,' she told him loftily. 'I was a Girl Guide —and a Ranger and I know how to do it . . .'

'I'm sure you do . . .'

'—But as it happened that huge creature there left behind a battered box containing four matches.' She shivered and he held her closer. 'Who is he anyway?'

'His name is Oso; he is the son of our old woodcutter. He has the mind of a child and in addition he is a deaf mute. Until now he has never done any sort of harm. But now he will have to go away.'

Luís's voice was flat and Jane knew better than to protest, though she could now feel sorry for the poor creature.

'It was my hair,' she shivered against Luís. 'He kept stroking my hair. It must have been he who watched me. I knew somebody was; I felt it.'

'Forgive me for doubting you—and for so many other things, Jane. I was such a fool . . .'

'We both did foolish things,' she told him, lovingly, looking back from the safety of his arms, so warm, so loving, so strong. She could tell by the way he held her how much she meant to him. 'But isn't that to be expected of people in love?'

She smiled up at him brimmingly and he kissed her then, holding her so tightly she could hardly breathe, but she made no protest; it was sheer luxury. When he let her go she laid her head against his shoulder.

'I am sorry I gave you so much worry,' she said apologetically. 'If I had not obeyed that last impulse to take a last look at the marble pool...' He tilted her chin so that he could look into her eyes.

'Oh, Jane, Jane...' he said in an odd voice, 'what have I done that I should find someone like you?'

'Why—just been you,' she said simply.

He drew her to him again and as she moved the chains clinked.

'Good God!' His voice vibrated with anger. 'I had forgotten he had you chained like an animal!'

'He treated me like one; he fed me and played with me and petted me... but I could not get through to him.'

Luís was examining the chains.

'We'll need a hammer and chisel or some steel cutters. I'll get...'

Then suddenly Jane was hurling herself past him and shouting: 'Look out, Luís...!' and he flung himself sideways and rolled away to see Oso up on one leg and coming at him again, fingers crooked. Jane flew at Oso but he swept her aside like a rag doll. She was thrown against the rock violently and hit her head. Luís kicked Oso's good leg from under him viciously and as he fell picked up the rifle and hit him as hard as he could on the head with the butt. Then he bent over Jane. Her head lolled back as he picked her up and from under the bright fall of hair the blood began to seep.

SEVEN

Jane opened her eyes. She was lying on her back in what she recognized after a moment as her own bed. Her head ached and she felt sore and stiff. It was night. The lamps were lit and the white voile curtains stirred ever so gently in a zephyr of a breeze.

Someone was holding her hand. Carefully she turned her aching head on the pillow to see Luís de Capdevila asleep in the chair by her bed. It was he who held her hand, fingers closely entwined, so that even in the total relaxation of sleep the clasp still held. At once, memory rushed back: the cave, the chains, the huge bulk of Oso coming at Luís, madness and hatred in his eyes. Her eyes flew over Luís anxiously. He did not appear hurt in any way. He was totally relaxed in the high-backed chair, having pulled it right by her bedside. He was still wearing the shirt and jeans he had worn when he found her in the cave and he had not shaved. All in all he was not his usual elegant self; he looked tired and strained and in need of the deep sleep in which he was held. She let her eyes dwell on his face as if she would never get enough of it. She smoothed her thumb gently over the long, lax fingers, but did not move her hand for fear of disturbing him.

She sighed contentedly. Everything was all right now.

Luís was here with her and he loved her. One look at his face when he found her in the cave was enough to tell her that nothing had changed; what he had said to her had confirmed it. He loved her. What had gone before was over and done with. They were together as they were meant to be.

Her heart was so full of love for him she thought it would burst. She loved the strong-boned face, the thick black hair, the dark eyes, the resonant, vibrant voice that could be so soft and caressing yet hard like steel. She loved the firm but sensual mouth, the hard jaw, the way its smile transformed his face, as it had when he had bent over her in the cave; a smile that was a conflagration of the most marvellous joy. In that moment she had committed herself to him all over again. She was his; whatever he wanted her to be, to do: just so long as she could be with him, yet somehow—instinctively, infallibly, she knew that what he wanted her to be was exactly what she was: independence, forthrightness, liberated ideas and all.

Drowsily content and secure she lay watching him, letting him sleep on, holding his hand, wanting—now anyway—nothing more than this, to be near him, with him, of him, so that the first thing she saw when he opened his eyes would be her.

And it was: when he awoke it was her face he saw, lying on the pillow smiling at him, all that she felt for him shining in those great green cat's eyes that had always been the window to her thoughts. She saw the answering gladness in his, and tightened her hold on his hand.

'My love,' she said softly.

In one fluid movement he was out of the chair and sitting on the bed, lifting her up to him, her arms going up about his neck. For a long moment they held each other without speaking. Then he said with a sigh: 'I thought he had killed you.'

'I thought he was going to kill *you*,' Jane's voice was muffled against his throat.

'You launched yourself at him like the wildcat I first saw in Madrid,' he said admiringly. 'Only he threw you against the wall with such force I thought you must have fractured your skull—but the blood was deceiving. You have a nasty cut though—does it hurt?'

'It aches,' she admitted, then with a mischievous glint in her eyes: 'But not enough to distract me from you.'

His response was to gather her even closer. 'From now on I will never let you out of my sight; I never want to go through another thirty-six hours like the last ones. I thought I had lost you, Jane—I mean really lost you. And again through my own stupidity and high-handedness.'

She put her fingers to his lips to silence them and he kissed them.

'No recriminations,' she admonished softly. 'We both made mistakes, but we won't make them again, will we?'

'Of course we will—but think of the delights there will be when we make it all up . . .'

After a while he looked down at her, his long fingers brushing away tendrils of hair from her forehead.

'We will fight like cat and dog,' he warned. 'But fighting with you is such a delight, and I would not have you any other way.' His regard was so fixed, so intense, that it shook her.

'I love you, Jane, so very much. I love your spirit and your gaiety and that effortless grace which touches everything you do; I love those green eyes and that quick, sharp tongue and your penetrating intelligence and loving appreciation of all things Spanish; I love the feel of you in my arms and the way you hold nothing back. I ask you to forgive me for hurting you so badly in a fit of stiff-necked pride; for believing lies when I knew—in spite of everything—that you were truth itself.'

Her eyes welled and again they exchanged a look so deeply probing that it touched the hearts and minds of both of them, and they could only cling tightly to each other. Jane pressed herself close against him her lips on the warm skin at the open neck of his shirt. He stroked her hair, kissing her softly and deeply, and with such tenderness that she was left weak and trembling. Then he kissed away the emotional tears from the corners of her eyes.

'I love you, I love you, I love you,' she whispered shakily. 'I think I will die of loving you.'

'What—and leave me a widower so soon?'

'You'll have to marry me first.'

'As soon as I can arrange it.'

'Oh, yes, please,' she begged, in such a voice as to make him kiss her again, this time with a passion that was all the more remarkable for being so ruthlessly controlled.

'I have made a lot of mistakes with you,' he said at last, his cheek against her hair. 'Like Jorge and the twins I have learned much this summer; you were something quite outside my experience—never mind Jorge's. You were at once a challenge and my defeat. From that first meeting when you turned on me, claws unsheathed . . .'

'We fought well, didn't we. I loved all that verbal fencing with you.'

'I had never met a woman with so much "*sal*".'

'The Señora told me you said I had "*sal*". I loved it. I loved you, and I thought—when you kissed me that night—that perhaps you loved me too . . .'

'I was beginning to and you were such a temptation! I had to use all my strength to resist you. I told you; you have an effect on a man that has to be experienced to be believed. I had never encounted anything like it and I knew that if I stayed I would not be able to keep my hands off you ... I had to remove myself before I violated every code in the book! Only I could not stay away. You became as necessary to me as breathing ...'

They kissed again, unable to get enough of each other. Then he said seriously: 'I would never chain you, Jane.' There was a smile in his voice lightening the underlying intensity. 'You are as free with me as you wish to be. I would not have you any other way.'

'But I am not free,' she said simply. 'I *am* chained to you, only you can't see them. And they can't be unlocked. Ever.'

He cupped her face in his hands and said to her what she had first said to him: 'My love.' Then he kissed her again, slow, deep kisses that had them both trembling.

Then he put her firmly back against the pillows.

'You must rest. I want you well soon, but if I have to marry you with a bandaged head I will do so.'

'Then kiss me some more,' she said promptly. 'It starts to ache when you don't.'

He laughed and her toes curled. 'Now I know you are on the mend,' he said dryly.

She clung to his hands. 'You will come back?'

'As soon as I have shaved and showered.'

Something struck Jane suddenly. 'Luís—have you sat by my bed all night?'

'Of course.'

She raised her arms to him but he got up. 'Oh, no,' he said. 'Leave me some vestige of free will.'

He took her hands and carried them to his mouth

palm upwards, kissing first one then the other, pressing the tip of his tongue against the warm skin. Her ears rang and she swallowed hard, perceiving, with a sensual thrill, just what sort of a lover this man would be.

'*Hasta pronto*,' he said. 'Until soon', and left her.

Left alone Jane raised her arms above her head and did her cat's stretch, every muscle cracking. They ached and her head throbbed but she felt so alive! So tinglingly, thoroughly, vibrantly alive!

Coming into the room the Señora said in surprise: '¡*Vaya!* For a young woman with a dozen stitches in her head you look remarkably well!'

'Stitches!' For the first time Jane put up a hand to feel the thick pad, the bandage. 'No wonder my head aches,' she said ruefully.

'It is not a bad wound, but jagged and deep enough to require stitches.'

'When was this—this morning—yesterday morning?'

'Two days ago.'

'Two days! Have I been unconscious all that time?'

'You were concussed. The doctor said it could be two days or two weeks. Luís was very worried.'

'And he has sat by my bed two days?'

'Ever since he brought you back. You were bleeding badly and it looked much worse than it finally turned out to be. But it was the concussion that worried us. You kept calling Luís and would not let go his hand. He held it all the time Dr Morales stitched you and has stayed with you ever since. I have never known him so distraught. He loves you very much. If I did not know him better I would say he is besotted.'

Jane looked shy suddenly. 'So am I.'

The Señora nodded happily. 'I can see that. He is as happy now as he was unhappy before. "I have been given another try," he said to me. "I don't know what I have done to deserve it having been such a fool but this time I will not let her go."'

'I never would,' Jane said simply. 'It was bad enough before when I thought all was lost: I could not go through that again.'

'I think he would have killed Oso if you had been seriously injured or if you had died,' the Señora said.

'What has happened to him?'

'He has been taken away where he will be looked after. He was never really dangerous, you understand. It was your hair which attracted him, like some pretty kitten. He wanted to stroke it and play with it. But it must have been very frightening.'

'It was. I never quite knew what to expect . . . how far he would go.'

'He did not—interfere—with you?' the Señora asked delicately.

'No. He never did more than stroke my hair.'

'The doctor said he did not think he had but it is as well to know. That is another reason Luís would have killed him.'

Jane shivered. 'I used to feel someone watching me. When I was on my own. It must have been Oso.'

'He knew all the estate very well. He was born here. But you must put it from your mind. Think of Luís . . .'

'I have been doing nothing else all summer,' confessed Jane guiltily.

'Oh, I knew that,' retorted the Señora. 'I could see how things were going with you two. Never has Luís come down to see us so often . . .'

She patted Jane's hand.

'He is very proud of you, you know. The way you lit the fire and got it smoking. "Whatever she does she does supremely well," he said to me.'

'Except for the bull,' Jane said with a shiver.

'Ah, well, that was something at which you had neither skill nor experience. That is why it was dangerous. Even a *tienta* is not really for novices.'

'I almost lost him over that,' Jane shuddered at the memory.

'He was afraid for you. What Queta did was unforgiveable. I knew that she hated you because of Luís but to go so far ...' The Señora was deeply shocked still. 'The lies she told Luís! He was bitterly ashamed for having believed them, but he had no reason to doubt her, you see.'

'Of course,' Jane said quietly. 'He had known her a long time.'

'All his life. And he trusted her. That is why he was so deep in despair when he went off to La Manja. He thought he had killed your love for him. But now—now he is a man transformed. He refused to leave you while you called for him.'

'I knew that if he was with me I was safe,' Jane said matter of factly.

'That is Luís,' agreed the Señora.

'He is so—so—' Jane could not find the English word. 'You have the right word in Spanish: *pundonor*. There was a time—one night in Cabo de los Angeles—I was in such a state he could have done whatever he wanted with me and I'd not have cared, but he said there were rules about that sort of thing.'

'Luís never cheats, and when he commits himself—and he had, I think, even then—it is even more important that he keeps to them. You impressed him from the start you know—when you flew at him that day in Madrid and lost your temper. "Such a rare one as that must not be allowed to get away," he told me, and he followed you out of the house. That in itself was most unusual! It was usually the women who followed Luís!' The Señora's chocolate eyes gleamed teasingly.

'He is a beautiful man, isn't he?' agreed Jane dreamily.

'Many women have thought so,' the Señora said innocently. 'But you had something that captured Luís: tremendous spirit. *"Tiene un valor enorme"*, he said. "She has enormous courage," and you stood by what you believed. That too, is important to him. And you gave as good as you got. He loved that too.'

The Señora smiled fondly at Jane. 'We all love you,' she said. 'My children were so unhappy when you were leaving us. Now they are overjoyed and they are all asking to see you. Do you feel up to it?'

'But of course! Please, let them come in.'

'Just five minutes, then.'

The twins hurtled through the door like stones from a catapult but pulled up short at the sight of her bandaged head.

'Oh, Miss Jane! You are injured!'

'Not badly. Only a cut on the head which will soon be better.'

'You were so white and your hair was all blood when Uncle Luís brought you back,' Inés said importantly. 'You looked dead. Luisíto and I both cried and went to the church and said prayers for you.'

'Which seem to have worked,' Jane said gravely, 'for I am alive and well as you see.'

'They took Oso away in an ambulance with bars on the windows,' Luisíto said in awed tones. 'He was crying.'

Jane held the twins close. 'He was not responsible for

his actions. He will be looked after where he has gone.'

'Is it true you are going to marry Uncle Luís? Lord James says you are.'

'Lord James is right. I am.'

'I'm glad,' Luisíto approved. 'Now you can stay with us always and you can help me look for more specimens when we get back to Cabo de los Angeles. Uncle Luís wants to take you there because he says it will do you good.'

'It is your Uncle Luís who does me good,' Jane said cheekily.

Jorge and Alejandro stood by her bed united in envious sorrow.

'So, it was *Tío* Luís all the time,' Jorge said reproachfully. 'No wonder you would not let me make love to you.'

'Or me,' echoed Alejandro. 'But it has been worth it to see Queta get her come uppance. Luís gave her hell.'

When James put his head round the door Jane held out her arms to him. 'Oh, James, James ... it has all turned out to be a kind of miracle; a sort of Lazarus affair. What I thought was dead is so overwhelmingly and splendidly alive and not only kicking but stampeding all over the place.'

'Hold on, there, young Jane, you don't have to tell me. I've seen and been talking to Luís! I'm to be best man. You approve?' He bent down to hug and kiss her.

'You *are* the best man—next to Luís, of course.'

'I take that as a compliment,' he said seriously. That's quite a man you've got there, love. I think even my old dad will approve—once he gets over his disappointment, of course. But what chance had I against a kidnapping and rescue by a handsome Spaniard?' He smiled at her wickedly. Then seriously: 'He was terribly worried, you know. He just did not sleep from the time you disappeared until you were brought back, treated by the doctor and pronounced out of danger. And even then he insisted on sleeping in the chair because whenever he let go of your hand you called for him. But he loved it. Wouldn't let anybody else take over—not even me!'

'I know,' Jane was shy suddenly, as if afraid of the size and depth of the love that had finally been revealed to her.

'I don't have to ask if everything is OK now. One look at you says it all; in spite of that bandaged head you still take one's breath away—And Luís is whistling like a ten-year-old. You have the most remarkable effect on him.' He eyed her quizzically and she blushed.

And then, there was Luís back again, bathed and shaved and back to his old elegance in beautifully cut black trousers and a pale blue shirt.

'Let me feast my eyes on you,' Jane told him lovingly.

'Likewise,' he answered softly.

Her hair had been brushed and dressed carefully, piled on top of her head to conceal the thick clump of bandage. She had put on her best nightdress and a lovely frothy-lace bedjacket the Señora had given her which just covered her broader shoulders but looked lovely against the honeyed apricot of her glowing skin, the gilt hair, the green eyes lit from within by a radiance that shone like a lamp in a window.

His own black hair was brushed and shining; the onyx eyes alight like her own, the dark face aglow with a look that poured over like a balm. He smelled of something sharp and clean.

'You are such a beautiful man,' she told him smugly, taking his hand, pulling him down to her, putting up a hand to trail fingertips down the high cheek bones to the firm jaw and smiling mouth, which kissed them as they went by.

'Marry me soon, Luís, before I die of longing,' she told him, with soft desolation.

With an exclamation he took her into his arms. 'Look at me like that and we will both die of exhaustion,' he warned her, his mouth against her throat.

She giggled. 'You smell nice,' she said, nuzzling him contentedly.

'So do you—and taste nice—and feel nice . . .'

'Our children will be distilled essence of us both,' she said after a while, dreamily.

'A potent mixture,' he commented dryly. 'If they have your beauty and grace and spirit I shall be content.'

'And your strength and integrity and those terrible dark eyes that can quell with one look.'

'As they did you?' he asked sardonically.

'It was because they did that I felt the need to assert myself,' she told him seriously.

'And you did; as a beautiful thorn in my flesh—so deep in my heart I will never be able to get you out.'

'Not even when I needle you?' she asked innocently, eyes brimful of laughter.

'Not even with that rapier you wield so well . . .'

She sighed again, well content.

'Then that's all right,' she said.

'My beautiful Amazon,' he smiled.

'Yes,' she said, offering him her mouth, her heart, her life. 'Yours.'